The *Right* CARD

DOROTHY ALEASE PHILLIPS

abbott press

Abbott Press books may be ordered through booksellers or by contacting:

Abbott Press
1663 Liberty Drive
Bloomington, IN 47403
www.abbottpress.com
Phone: 1 (866) 697-5310

Because of the dynamic nature of the Internet, any web addresses or links contained in this book may have changed since publication and may no longer be valid. The views expressed in this work are solely those of the author and do not necessarily reflect the views of the publisher, and the publisher hereby disclaims any responsibility for them.

Any people depicted in stock imagery provided by Getty Images are models, and such images are being used for illustrative purposes only. Certain stock imagery © Getty Images.

Scripture quotations are from the King James Version of the Bible.

ISBN: 978-1-4582-2295-4 (sc)
ISBN: 978-1-4582-2294-7 (e)

Library of Congress Control Number: 2020920055

Print information available on the last page.

Abbott Press rev. date: 12/03/2020

Dedicaton

The Lord, Himself, must have been the "Match Maker" for my two sons, Dean Hayward Phillips and Kent Vincent Phillips; for both chose intelligent, beautiful, Christian girls to be their wives.

Dean's wife Marilyn was the daughter of a Baptist minister. Rev. James Harris and his wife Carolyn; Kent's wife, the daughter of foreign missionaries, Dr. Keith and Nurse Alice Edwards.

Marilyn and Marianne have been true daughters to me. I love both dearly. They have made great mothers and "super" grandmothers. Their children rise up and call them *blessed*. I say, "Amen" to that.

Acknowledgements

"Behind the Scenes" people are great. They help to keep things running smoothly. Authors, who struggle with cantankerous computers and word processors that have minds of their own, frequently slip aside and let expert technicians take over.

Over the years, I have been blessed with acquaintances who are pros in their fields. I have, thankfully, enjoyed their assistance.

For **The Right Card,** I offer special thanks to Rev. Mark Abbott and Mr. Dick O'Driscoll for their computer expertise. For manuscript handling and telephone messaging, I laud Cindy O'Driscoll and Mashica Robinson.

Thank you, Dear Ones, for your ready, efficient help. You have been a blessing.

Preface

As a high school teacher and a minister's wife, I eased into a position just right for me. I automatically became a "Match Maker." (I remembered how my dad, as a barber, earned the title of "Employment Placer." At his funeral, many often said to a family member, "Mr. Hicks got me my job." Daddy knew the needs and he knew the right people to fill needs.) Now, as for me, I earned the reputation for getting people sweethearts and mates. Perhaps, that is why I'm happy to write a love story. I believe in love – sometimes at first sight; at other times, after a growth period that allows two people to get to know each other.

The Right Card follows the rocky courtship of a young minister who is praying for a wife but constantly facing hindrances.

Chapter 1

udith Johnson had browsed the card counter for almost fifteen minutes, reading an assortment of birthday cards. Now, lingering at the humorous section, she smiled as she read a series of comical verses. Holding a card shaped like an hour-glass woman, suddenly she laughed. Aware of her outburst, she glanced around to see if anyone had heard. She was startled to see a tall, young man standing six feet away with arms crossed loosely across his chest, looking at her with a bemused smile.

"Oh, my," she said, "I didn't mean to laugh aloud, but this one is funny." As he approached her, she handed him the card. "See if you don't think it's funny."

As he read the card, Judith gave a quick, examining glance. *Tall and handsome. Dignified. Stylish, grey suit. White shirt. Maroon tie.* She wanted to put her hand over her heart; for, strangely, it began beating rapidly. She did not move.

Having read the card, the stranger laughed. "You 're right," he said. This is funny."

Another quick assessment. *Beautiful white teeth and a smile that brought a dimple to his right cheek.*

Compelled to give an explanation, Judith said, "I'm looking for cards for my mother's birthday next week. I have this little oddity: I always give her two cards – one that is humorous and one that is sentimental. I like for her to have a good laugh but then I like for her to know how much I treasure her."

"I like this humorous card," the young man said. "Is there another one like it? I need a card for my mother. too."

Smiling, Judith took down another similar card.

He moved closer and said, "By the way, my name is Scott Jacobs, and you are?

"Judith Johnson," she said and extended her hand.

He took her hand to shake but did not let it go. "Now, Judith Johnson, since we have been introduced, I need to ask you something." He paused; her heart raced. With mocked seriousness he asked, "Will you marry me?"

Judith laughed and answered, "Yes, but it will have to be after next week, for I have a lot of papers to grade."

"So, you are a teacher. That is perfect." Scott said. "I'm a minister. I pastor the Community Church in Zilford just 35 miles away. Preachers and teachers make great combinations, you know."

Judith smiled and turned away. "I need to pick out my sentimental card. Look at this," she said. "I had almost settled for this one earlier."

"I like it," he said. "Give me one like that. Incidentally, when is your mother's birthday?"

"October, the seventh," she said.

"Can you believe it," he said with amusement. "My mother's birthday is October, the seventh! Now, that just goes to show you that we should get married; we would never forget our mothers' birthdays."

Judith laughed.

As they paid for their cards, Scott said, "Judith Johnson, would you go to Starbuck's with me for a cup of coffee?"

She hesitated, looking at her watch. "I'm going shopping with my mother at two o'clock."

Scott looked at his watch. "Good. That gives us plenty of time for two or three cups of coffee and a dozen sweet rolls too."

When Scott touched her elbow as he escorted her across the street, Judith was aware of his nearness, his cologne, his manliness.

Over coffee, the two learned much about each other. Sometimes they chuckled; sometimes they spoke with quite seriousness.

She was an only child. He had two brothers and one sister.

Her widowed mother lived near her. His parents lived 200 miles away.

She had taught senior English for two years. He had been pastor of the Community Church for a year. It was his first pastorate.

At length, Scott looked at Judith and said quietly, "You know when I was praying early this morning, I told the Lord I needed a wife. I, also, told Him some things I wanted in a wife, and one thing I prayed was, 'Lord, if it can be your will, please give a wife with a keen sense of humor.' When I saw you giggling over those cards, I said, 'Lord, I didn't know you were going to answer me so quickly.' That's why I asked you to marry me. Now, I'm not going to ask you again at this time because I know you have papers to grade, but I truly believe I will ask you again."

Judith smiled and surprised herself by saying, "I'll hold you to that so that; someday I may tell our children and grandchildren that you asked me to be your wife the first time you saw me.

He reached across the table and said, "Let's shake on that." He added, "I have one other request." He covered their two hands with his free hand. "Could we name our first son Jude Jacobs? Jude after you and Jacobs after me. Jude Jacobs. That sounds good. It would be a good biblical name for a pro quarterback."

Judith shook her head and laughed. *This wonderful man. How much fun it would be to be his wife.*

Before they left the table, Jacob removed a small, leather book from his jacket. "Give me your telephone number, Judith. I will be calling you." He wrote down her number and reached for the check.

"Judith, there is one other thing I need to say. I flirted with you today, didn't I?"

"Yes, you did; but did you notice: I flirted back?"

Scott chuckled. "I'm glad you did. Only, to me, it did not seem that we were flirting. Our light conversation was such a natural thing; but I must admit, it was out of character for me. You see, I'm very careful around women – seminary training, you know. I never, never flirt. I do not take women to ride in my car. I do not visit in a home where a young lady is alone. I have all the safety guards. Now, how do we account for what happened today?"

"Maybe, it's because you prayed this morning, and I have been praying for the right husband since I was 12 years old, and you did ask me to marry you."

They both laughed, and Scott said, "Good answer; and now, Judith Johnson, I'll walk you to your car."

Scott drove below the speed limit on the way to Zilford. He wanted time to think about Judith Johnson. Her beauty. Her hair. It made him think of writers who had compared girl's hair to corn silk. Now he understood. The description was just right for Judith's hair, blonde with streaks of beige and gold. Her eyes were blue, a blue unlike the blue of his eyes. His eyes were a gray blue; but hers, a clear light blue.

He remembered how she answered when he, teasingly asked, "In the last two years, what has happened in your life to bring you great joy?" She had lowered her lashes and said, "I know, but I can't tell you." She fingered the little cross hanging around her neck.

"Why?" he said. "Was it something illegal or sinful?"

"Oh, nothing like that. It is just that I would rather someone else told you."

"There is no one else; so, Judy, if I may call you Judy, you will have to tell me. What made you happy?"

Seemingly, she debated answering; but then she shrugged her shoulders and smiling said quietly, "I was voted 'Teacher of the Year' two years in a row. I'm sure I did not deserve it, but I was happy because my fellow teachers honored me that way. Now, in all fairness, Scott (if I should call you Scott and not Preacher), you must tell me what has made you happy in the last two years."

"I can do that easily," Scott replied. "I finished college and received a call to pastor the Zilford Community Church. For a year and two months, I have had the privilege to lead a congregation of wonderful people. Did I tell you? I love being a preacher and pastoring a church."

"I'm sure you are a super preacher." She touched his arm and added, "By the way, did I tell you? I love teaching." They both smiled.

In his rearview mirror, Scott saw a car approaching and moved over to the right lane. He had been riding in the left lane only when there was no other traffic. He was in no hurry. He was enjoying driving leisurely, remembering the afternoon spent with Judith Johnson.

Judith had finished college. That was good. She loved her work and that was good.

On impulse, Scott took a Rest Area exit, pulled into a remote parking space, turned off the motor, and began to pray. "Father," he said. I need to talk with you about what has happened in the last few hours. I'm concerned about my behavior. You know how careful I've always been. Since high school, I've sought your leadership in setting up standards for my life. Today, I met a young woman and I'm puzzled by my behavior. It's weird, but from the moment I saw Judith Johnson, I felt as though I had known her all my life. Now, Father, you know that I prayed about a wife early this morning. Genesis records you said it was not good for man to live alone and you gave Adam a helpmate. Today, I asked you for a helpmate. I need to know. Is Judith Johnson the helpmate you have picked for me? It's just so very strange that, this very day, we met as we did and felt so very at ease with each other. You know, Father, I have never engaged in such frivolous chitchat with a stranger before." He continued his talk with the Lord for several minutes and then sat quietly to let the Lord speak to his heart. At length, he pulled out onto the highway.

He stopped at Zilford's main red light. The hub of the little 25,000 city was always alive on Saturdays. He rode slowly down Main Street, watching for people crossing the streets, still thinking about Judith. Judy to him. She was just the right height; the top of her head reached the top of his shoulders. And then he thought of her quick wit. He liked that she had mentioned telling their children and grandchildren about his speedy proposal.

He turned into the long driveway that led to the Community Church, a cream-colored brick building nestled back amid a grove of huge oak trees. As he drove into the main parking lot, he was surprised to see several cars parked near his office. There was Dr. Gilham's car, Fred Barnell's new Cadillac, Mitch Morgan's Buick, Josh Morton's new truck; Ken Harmon's Town car; and two other vehicles he could not identify.

Dr. Gilham met him at the door.

"Hi, Dr. Gilham," Scott said with a smile as he extended his hand. Dr. Gilham neither responded to the greeting nor the handshake."

"When you have hung up your coat," he said curtly, the deacons would like to see you in the conference room."

Scott wanted to ask what was up, but Dr. Gilham turned and walked down the hall.

Suddenly, Scott felt a foreboding, a sinking feeling. He could not imagine what was wrong. The church was thriving. Each week new people were coming into the fellowship, and he could think of no great problem.

As he entered the conference room, he noted that Dr. Gilham walked to the head of the table where he, as the pastor, had always sat. Three men sat on each side of the table, leaving one empty chair.

At first, he did not sit. "Gentlemen," he said, "what's going on?"

Dr. Gilham seated himself in the main chair. "We are here to talk to you about…about you."

Stunned, Scott felt as though someone had punched him in the stomach. It was the same kind of feeling he had experienced the first time a lineman had plowed into his mid-section. "I do not understand," he said.

"Sit down and we will explain," Dr. Gilham said. The other deacons sat still except for mild-mannered Ken Harmon. He squirmed in his seat and lowered his head. Dr. Gilham began a stern rebuke. "We are not pleased with your leadership in our church."

Scott could not speak.

"For the past several weeks you have been preaching, what we consider, unacceptable sermons. We are here to say that unless you make some changes, we are prepared to ask you to resign."

In disbelief, Scott gulped. He said, "I do not understand. Our congregation is growing with every service. And you men know that we added sixty-five people to our membership this past year."

"That has nothing to do with our complaint." Dr. Gilham said. "If we get them, it is our job to see that we keep them. Your preaching will eventually drive them away."

Scott's mind raced to the three times in the past week that church families had told him that he was the best preacher they had ever heard. Elderly Ben Barnes had declared that he was a better preacher than Billy Graham. Scott always paid little attention to such comments, but he did appreciate kind encouragements.

"I spend a lot of time preparing my sermons," the young minister said. "I do a lot of research and I try to make my sermons interesting."

Ken Harmon dared to speak out. "You are a good speaker, Son. No one is saying that."

Dr. Gilham, a Duke graduate who usually exalted himself above other Community Church laymen, gave a scolding glance to Mr. Harmon, and once again Mr. Harmon squirmed in his seat and lowered his head.

"I'm afraid you are going to have to be more specific," Scott said, regaining an inner composure. He stood up, his six feet-four-inch frame facing the arrogant doctor.

"Very well. We do not like your last series of messages," Dr. Gilham said, slightly intimidated by Scott's sudden sense of control.

"Now, let me see," Scott said. "I have been preaching a series of messages on the Ten Commandments. Am I to understand you men do not believe in the Ten Commandments?"

The other deacons spoke up. " No." "No, nothing like that. We believe in the Ten Commandments."

"What then?" Scott asked. "Was there error in what I taught?"

"No," Dr. Gilham said. "Dr. Jarmon, our former pastor, did not preach the way you do. He was a scholar and never stooped to stress certain things. For instance, last week you said things you could have left unsaid."

"Last week? Last Sunday, if I remember right, I preached on the seventh commandment. Did I not use good discretion in handling the subject of adultery and fornication? I tried to keep in mind the women and children in our audience, but, as your pastor, I am commanded to preach the whole counsel of God."

"You may need to preach the whole counsel, but you went too far when you said that pre-marital sex and extra-marital sex are sins. Not everyone agrees with that."

"That's right," Mitch Morton, who was a known philanderer, blurted out and then looked embarrassed by his own comment.

"What does the Bible say?" Scott asked.

"We know what the Bible says," Fred Barnell said ."but sometimes you have used the pulpit to meddle in things that are not your business.

"I'm sorry you feel that way. I'm very careful to stick to what scripture says on any issue, Brother Fred."

Dr. Gilham interrupted. "We didn't bring you here today to hear you preach," he said angrily. "You either hear us and change what you are doing or you will be asked to resign one month from now."

Scott narrowed his eyes. "Do you think this is what the church body wants?"

Still acting as the sole spokesman, Dr. Gilham responded, "We are the Deacon Board of Community Church, and we make the decisions." He emphasized the word, "we."

He placed his two hands down on the desk and looked up at Scott in defiance "Now, we have said what we want to say and you are excused."

Scott paused, wondering if he should say more. He gazed around the table at the men who, a year ago, had invited him to pastor the Community Church. Most of the men avoided eye contact. It was then that he felt the divine leadership of the Lord. "Good evening, gentlemen," he said calmly and left the room.

In the parking lot, Scott wanted to put his head down on the steering wheel to release the hurt bottled within, but he knew he could not do that. Some of the men were exiting the church. A loud rapping against his window startled Scott. He turned to see Dr. Gilham glaring at him. "Roll down the window," he demanded. "I want to talk to you."

"Would you like to get into the car?" Scott said.

"Yes, I will do that," Dr. Gilham said, going around the car. Once seated, he said, "Jacobs, I suppose you know that one family did not vote for you to come to our church as pastor. Well, that was my family. Would you like to know why I was opposed to electing you?"

"Only if you wish to tell me," Scott said.

"Well, I'll tell you and I can prove I was right. I didn't want to hire an unmarried man. I knew a single man would be too mixed up with women. Well, today you proved me right. I saw you in Starbucks holding hands with some blonde. Not in our town, mind you, but off where no one could see you. Who was she? Some cheap little 'nothing' you met in Cantrell?"

"Absolutely not," Scott said, feeling a surge of anger, an anger he had not felt since his little sister's arm was broken by Butch Jones. "Judith Johnson is an outstanding teacher at Cantrell High As a matter of fact, she has been selected "Teacher of the Year" for the last two years."

"Judith Johnson?" Dr. Gilham said. Scott groaned within. Why had he mentioned her name? With a smirk, Dr. Gilham said, "Well, well. The principal of Cantrell High happens to be a good friend of mine. I think I should talk with him about his prized teacher."

Scott turned abruptly to face Dr. Gilham. "Sir, you may say anything to me or about me; but I warn you, you are not to say anything about Judith Johnson." He hated himself for calling her name again. "You leave that fine teacher out of this."

"That's up to you," Dr. Gilham said with a grin. He stepped outside and slammed the door.

On the way to the parsonage, fear and dismay engulfed Scott. How he wished his mother and father were there to counsel him and to pray with him. He had always treasured their Godly guidance. Now, he dreaded going into an empty house.

As he entered the door, he whispered, "Judy, how I wish you were here. I do hope I have not caused you any trouble."

Chapter 2

Judith Johnson beamed, thinking about the handsome man
the Lord had sent her way. Scott Jacobs was a gift-wrapped
answer to prayers. Since her father's death, as an only child,
she had dedicated her life to her mother. Even though she had
her own apartment and many obligations, as a daughter, she put
everything aside to spend time with her mother. They ate and
went places together. Judy tried to fill the void in her mother's life.
With so much time given to her mother and to pressing teaching
duties, of necessity, she dropped dreams of marriage and children.
Then, she met Scott Jacobs. Within minutes, it was as though they
had always known each other. They laughed, talked, and shared
innermost thoughts. She felt as though this initial meeting was
the beginning of a lifetime commitment.

At least, this was the way Judith felt for a day or two; but
when the phone did not ring, she became concerned. Had she
only imagined that Scott felt the same way that she felt? Was
the attractive Scott Jacobs merely a "ladies' man" who charmed
many women along the way? Perhaps, in his church there were
numerous women who had succumbed to his magnetism. Yet,
she could not believe this.

Judith had always prided herself on being a good judge of
character; her father had claimed she had inherited that trait

from him. Now, she began to wonder. Even though she was a respected high school teacher, was she as easily gullible to romantic enchantment as her whimsical students were? Did she read more into this accidental meeting than she should have? Was Scott Jacobs a man of character or was he a charlatan whom she had misjudged? She was glad that she had not shared her unusual meeting with Scott with anyone; for, now, she would feel foolish. *Dear Lord, only you and I know about Scott Jacobs and how I feel. Please give me wisdom and leadership.*

At times at night, she awoke suddenly with a deep impression to pray for Scott Jacobs. Although she was hurt that she had been snubbed by this man, still she felt compelled to call his name to the Lord. She prayed for him daily. *Father, I do not know why I feel the urge to pray for Scott Jacobs, but he comes to mind so very often. Please. If he has a need, meet it. He is a minister of the gospel, but he is very young. He may be, especially, in need of your guidance at this time. Bless him I pray.*

Going to church became a burden for Scott, not because he did not love the members of his flock but because he could not know who loved him and who judged him as the Deacon Board had. He knew that almost everyone greeted him warmly in the hallways and in the vestibule after church. Only the deacons and some of the members of their families seemed to shy away. Almost everyone left by his door after each service to voice words like "That was a great message, Pastor" or "That sermon was a blessing, Brother Scott." Of the deacons, however, only Ken Harmon left by the main door; the other deacons took side exits.

Dr. Gilham had started an unusual behavior; he had begun bringing a briefcase to church, a thing he had not done before. Every time that Scott saw Dr. Gilham walking the halls with his briefcase by his side, he wondered if the doctor was collecting depositions or circulating petitions.

During the church services, Dr. Gilham, Mitch Morgan, and Fred Barnell had begun sitting at the back of the church where they often whispered or wrote notes. Ken Harmon still sat with his wife and three children several pews from the front in the center section. Josh Morton had begun missing services; his family came without him and made excuses. The other three deacons who had sat quietly during the devastating discussion still came to church but avoided speaking with the pastor.

Scott spent much time in prayer, asking the Lord for leadership. He felt no urge to leave his pastorate; and yet, he knew Dr. Gilham had put him on trial for one month. Unless he had divine leading, Scott was certain that he could not, nor would not, change his method of preaching. He reasoned within himself that he was considered to be intelligent, rational, and well trained; but these were not the attributes upon which he depended; more than ever he now relied upon a close communion with the Lord.

Daily he spent time searching the Scriptures and writing down verses that pertained to God's promised leadership. Often he said aloud, *Trust in the Lord with all thine heart; and lean not unto thine own understanding. In all thy ways, acknowledge him, and he shall direct thy paths.* At home, he paced the floor, talking with the Lord. At church, he slipped into the sanctuary and knelt at the altar or walked up and down, touching each pew and praying for those who would sit there. His heart was always heavy when he stopped at the pew where Dr. Gilham had begun sitting. *Father, I do not know how to reach this man, but I look only on the outside; you see the heart. Give me wisdom to understand Dr. Gilham....and, please, give me the ability to love him and to rise above the hurt I am now feeling.*

He stayed longer at that pew than at other pews.

hapter 3

In Cantrell Central High where Judith taught, there were two other single teachers – Zack Matson, who taught speech and journalism, and Mike Moring, who taught history and social studies. Both teachers were a year or two older than Judith and often vied for her attention. Judith liked both young men as friends but so far she had consented only to a cup of coffee in the school cafeteria or a walk around the track area early in the morning or after school. She had refused other invitations.

Perhaps it was because of her recent Scott Jacobs' disappointment that she finally agreed to go with Zack to tryouts at the Community Theater.

"Come on, Judith," he had coaxed. "The theater is going to present *Our Town* and you know you have to cover that play every year in American literature."

Because he was right and her eleventh-grade students had just acted out the play in class, she considered his request.

"I'm going," Zack explained, "because they have asked me to take the part of the Stage Manager. At first I said, 'No,' but I reread the play and decided I would like the challenge – just to see if I have the ability to memorize again.

"Zack, you will be great for that part; you will be the ideal narrator. Your voice will be perfect!" He did have the deepest, most melodious voice she had ever heard. She had often thought that she would love to hear him read Elizabeth Barrett's sonnet, "How do I love thee? Let me count the ways," or Edgar Allan Poe's "The Raven" or "The Bells." If she went with him this evening to the tryouts, she would have a chance to hear him read.

"I still have to try out but I believe I have the job." Then he grinned and added, "Go with me and give me moral support just in case."

Judith thought for a moment. She was headed toward her usual evening in a lonely apartment with papers to grade and lesson plans to review but, all the while, secretly waiting for her phone to ring. She looked up at Zack and said, "Why not? Yes, why not! What time shall I be ready?"

"The tryouts start at 7 o'clock. I was wondering if you would like to go with me to the Red Lobster at five for some seafood. Then you would not have to cook supper," he added, hoping to entice her. Always, before when he had asked, she had nicely turned him down.

It's a date." Judith surprised him by saying. " I haven't had Red Lobster's cheese biscuits in a long time; and, luckily, my mom is going out with some friends this evening."

"Good!" he said as he clasped her hand. Then he turned and strolled away, looking back to give her a smile.

Judith stood, watching him depart and, for once, allowed herself to appreciate his handsomeness. His thick black, curly hair. His broad shoulders. His unique, quick stride. No wonder the twelfth-grade girls had a crush on this young teacher.

The evening meal was delightful. Away from school, Judith found that she could easily talk with Zack. They had many things in common. Their families. Their hometown high schools. Their love for reading.

It was almost disappointing when Zack glanced at his watch and realized it was almost time for "the showdown" as he called it. "Time to go," he said, going behind her chair to help her rise.

The auditorium was filled with all ages, for the play called for many characters. The Stage Manager's part was considered first; but after Zack Matson read, the other aspiring Stage Managers declared they needed to try for other roles. Zack was without doubt the choice actor for that part.

Dr. Gibbs and Mrs. Gibbs were selected next. Then Mr. Webb and Mrs. Webb were chosen. The auditions were moving along smoothly. A young State Community College teacher, Robert Street, read for the role of young George Gibbs and was given the part immediately.

The director checked his clipboard. "Now, it is time to hear those of you who are trying out for Emily Webb. I see the first name on the list is Judith Johnson." He glanced up. Judith started to protest. She had no intention of trying out for a part. She surely had not submitted her name. She opened her mouth to speak but Zack stopped her.

"Here she is, Mr. Graham. Go on, Judith," he said giving her a nudge. "Why not?" he whispered to her. Judith's first inclination to be angry subsided as Zack stood, stepped aside, and bowing as an usher, encouraged her to follow him. She rolled her eyes. "Why not indeed?" she mumbled.

It seemed it had been a long time since she had done something rash on impulse, but Zack made it easy. Smiling, she mounted the steps to the stage and was asked to begin reading where Emily asked, "Mama, am I good-looking? Someone voiced the mother's answer and Emily continued, "Oh, Mama, that's not what I mean. What I mean is: Am I pretty?" She had read only a few more lines when the director stopped her and said, "Well,

I think we have found our Emily. Let's move on to Rebecca Gibbs."

With her hand clasped across her mouth, Judith returned to her seat, welcomed by a grinning Zack Matson. She shook her head in disbelief. Everything had happened so very quickly. It had hardly registered that she was to have the leading part in a play when Robert Street made his way to her. "Hello, Emily. You and I are going to love each other in this play, you know. You're going to be my wife."

Perhaps it was the release of the hour's tryout emotions, for Judith responded, "Yes, I'm going to be your wife, but I'm going to die Now, isn't that sad? Isn't there something you can do about that?"

Robert Street was only a few inches taller than she, but he looked like a mythical god. He had wavy, blond hair and bronze skin. He was muscular He swaggered with confidence. She knew immediately that he was absolutely sure of himself.

"I'll rewrite the play if you will marry me," he said.

Zack interrupted, "Sorry to break this up, but I must get this lady home. She told me she has papers to grade, and 6 o'clock tomorrow morning will come quickly."

Judith reached for the coat draped over her chair. Both men attempted to help her, but Robert eyed Zack and stood back. He said, "Well, goodnight, Emily. I'll see you in rehearsal."

Rehearsal? That was something Judith had not thought of. Now it became a concern. In his opening speech, the director had warned that for the next five weeks rehearsals would be held every evening, except Sunday, from 7:00 until 10:30. No one would be excused. Could she possibly keep up with her school work and give this much time to rehearsing? What if? Oh, yes, what if Scott Jacobs called? This demeaning thought helped her make up her mind. She would accept the challenge. She would dedicate her time to five weeks of rehearsals. She would do the best she could with her role as Emily, and she would turn her answering machine off!

Maybe she had found a way to get Scott Jacobs out of her mind.

Chapter 4

Many people showed kindnesses to Scott. Little Widow Brown cooked him some collard greens, apple turnovers, or blueberry muffins – much the way his mother had prepared them. He smiled when she brought him collards, for she always promised him she washed them four times. Often, she invited him for a home-cooked meal. As for other homes, he ate with the Petersons the most, for the Petersons were the family that met him at the airport when he came for a trial weekend Since then, he had been in their home almost weekly.

The Peterson family consisted of Mr. and Mrs. Peterson; Mrs. Peterson's widowed mother, Mrs. Ashton; a 20-year-old daughter, Debbie; and a 12 year-old son, Philip. Debbie was away in college when Scott first met the Peterson family and he had seen her only once in church with her family.

He was pleased when he arrived at the Peterson home for dinner one Saturday evening and Debbie answered the door bell, swinging wide the door and saying, "Come in, Pastor Jacobs. The steaks are almost ready." She flipped her long black hair over her shoulder and looked up at him with deep blue eyes. As she smiled up at him, he was amazed at the similarity of this young lady and his sister. They were the same height, same size, and had the same color of hair and eyes. Debbie's voice was, also, soft and musical just like Gillian's. He had a strange longing to put his arms around her and to hug her just as he always did his little sister.

Mr. Peterson came down the stairs, buttoning his sweater. "Hi, Pastor," he said. "We're glad you can eat with us tonight. We're celebrating Debbie's birthday, don't you know?

"No, I didn't know," Scott said. "Look. I came empty handed."

"That's fine," Mr. Peterson said, putting his arm around Debbie's shoulder. "My little girl's no longer a teenager and she's not happy about that. I don't believe she wanted us to tell anyone."

Maybe that had been true; but as Debbie looked at the striking Scott Jacobs, she changed her mind. She was glad she was older. She could even wish to add a year or two.

During the meal, conversation came easy. Together, Debbie and her "little brother," as she called him, kept everyone entertained. Scott became mindful of what he had been missing for the past year. Mealtimes in his parents' home had always been happy and meaningful. Now, he realized a fact: one of the hardest things he had faced since being in Zilford was having to eat his meals alone.

In seminary, Scott had been taught not to spend too much time with any "one family" in his church. His professor had warned that other church members would be jealous. Up until now, he had tried to follow that advice by spreading his visits to as many homes as possible, showing no certain-family preference; but now a change came. The Petersons were inviting him, even more than usual, to eat with them or to go with them somewhere, and he was finding it difficult to turn down their invitations.

Without anyone mentioning it, Scott began to wonder if the Petersons had learned about his dilemma at church. Had

Dr. Gilham or one of the other deacons approached this family? Were the Petersons seeking to compensate for his behind-the-scene troubles? No matter why they were showering him with love and concern, Scott was grateful. He needed the closeness of a family.

For the next three weeks, he ate with the Petersons each Sunday. It was strange, but Debbie came home every weekend now. She flounced around the house, laughing and chatting, creating a happy, carefree atmosphere. Her family adored her; Scott could tell, for Mr. Peterson, as well as the other family members, were often seen giving Debbie an affectionate hug.

Scott watched and mused. What a joy Debbie brought to her home. She was beautiful, thoughtful, and cheerful, always bounding with energy. To him, it was as though his own little sister had been transplanted to Zilford.

Yes, Debbie Peterson was special. He enjoyed being near her; yet, Debbie, with her unique appeal, did not keep him from thinking about Judith Johnson. He longed to phone her....to explain why he had not called, but he could not do that. He remembered Dr. Gilham's threat to speak to his friend, the principal. Often he prayed, *Father, I cannot get Judith in trouble. She does not deserve to suffer because of me. Protect her, please.*

Too, he dismissed the idea of sharing what had happened at the unscheduled deacons' meeting. How could he explain Dr. Gilham's "or-else" ultimatum after he had given Judith such a glowing report about his church? Even he, himself, could not understand how or why all this had happened. The church was doing so very well. The congregation was growing with each service and the people seemed happy. He had watched families coming in with their Bibles, taking notes, fellowshipping with each other. His heart had been warmed by kind comments and friendly handshakes.

Of necessity, Judith had to organize every minute of her day. She needed to allot time for her school responsibilities, play rehearsals, church activities; and her daily contact with her mother. In the past, to spend as much time as possible with Mrs. Johnson, Judith had taken her mother out for dinner at least three times a week. Each evening they had visited a different restaurant, sampling various cuisines. Then, in accordance with her mother's wishes, she always went to her mother's home twice a week for a home-cooked meal.

Thus, weeks flew by with Judith Johnson racing through hectic, packed days. She was surprised, from time to time, that the Community Church pastor suddenly crossed her mind. She could not understand why she thought of him; Scott Jacobs had been a cad who promised to call her but had not. Such behavior was inexcusable. And besides, why should she care? She was beginning to feel like Scarlet O'Hara with a bevy of eligible young men clamoring for her attention. She willed herself not think about Scott Jacobs.

Rehearsal time was well spent. Showing no intimidation because of his cast of teachers and other professionals, Director Rob Hagan was in complete control. He blocked out each scene, instructed action, and questioned actors' interpretations at times; but at the same time, freely gave praise when deserved.

Judith enjoyed every practice even when she was not in a scene. Having heard her students read *Our Town,* she delighted now in hearing the better-trained actors interpret familiar lines. She knew she would encourage all of her students to attend the play.

On stage, Judith relished the challenge of acting. She was thankful that she could be Emily, and she was equally thankful that handsome Robert Street was George. Often the two were sent aside to read their lines together. She loved Robert's deep, resonant voice as he spoke his lines to her.

Robert's appearance was different from that of any young men that Judith knew. He had blond hair and bushy eyebrows of the same color. In contrast, his complexion was a golden bronze. His bluish-green eyes constantly twinkled with merriment. Sometimes, Judith wondered how he would ever change such laughing eyes to look sad during the death scenes.

Often Robert and Zack sat with her when they were not on stage. Both men were comics. At times, when they were on stage, it was difficult to keep composure when one of them made an under-breath remark or chuckled over an unintentional pun.

"Guys," Judith said, "we are all teachers. How can we be acting like our cut-up students?"

"It's easy," Robert said. "We've learned from the experts."

"Anyway, we are all health conscious; and everyone knows, that according to the Bible, laughter is good like medicine," Zack added. "We're going to be extremely healthy."

Constantly, the three joked, using titles or wordings from literary works. For instance, when a prop fell with a thud, Zack whispered, "The Fall of the House of Usher." At another time, when the director instructed Daniel Kilman to change the way he walked across the stage, Robert muttered, "The Devil and Daniel Webster."

"Judith," Robert said one evening after rehearsal, "let's get a bite to eat. It's early, and I promise you will get home at a good hour."

"I'll have to call to ask my mother if it's all right," Judith joked.

"Go ahead," he said. "I'll wait. Tell her, though, that she will like me. Most mothers usually do."

Judith was busy putting on her coat, considering the invitation when Zack came up and gave her a similar invitation. Looking at the two as she pulled on her gloves, Judith said, "Fiddle dee dee, Boys, I need to get back to Tara." She really did need to leave.

Zack said, "Miz Scarlet, you surely take the joy of life away from us."

The three laughed, walked to the parking lot together, and rode away in separate cars.

Chapter 5

Scott Jacobs determined that, with the help of the Lord, he would live above the hurtful stress thrust upon him. He kept a rigid schedule. Each weekday, he arose at seven o'clock and arrived at the church by eight. As usual, he called the staff together for a brief time of sharing needs and goals. He read scripture and prayed with his co-workers before they went to their separate offices. Then he began his private devotional time, an hour of Bible study and prayer for his congregation. Since the church members knew that their pastor dedicated this hour to prayer and study, they usually called him at another time. Unless it was necessary, the secretary did not interrupt him while the study door was closed. Early one day, however, his secretary tapped on the door When Scott called, "Come in," she opened the door and whispered, "Pastor, Granny Hansley is on the line and she is crying. She seems very upset."

Scott reached for the phone and said softly, "Hello, Granny Hansley. How can I help you?" Everyone called the Community Church's oldest member "Granny." She wanted them to do so.

"Oh, Pastor," the little 90-year-old lady cried. "I have waited for three months for my appointment with my doctor. I really need to see him, but I can't find anyone to take me to Cantrell.

What am I going to do? I can't pay for a cab to take me 35 miles." Again he could hear her crying.

"There. There," Scott said. "You have a way. I'll take you. You just tell me when to come for you." He sought to comfort her further, "We'll have a good time of fellowship, riding to Cantrell. You know, you still have a lot to tell me about the years you lived in Alaska."

"Oh, thank you. Thank you, Pastor I didn't mean for you to have to take me, but I thought you could tell me what to do. Now that I am all alone, sometimes I'm at a loss. My children used to make so very many decisions for me." He heard Granny sniffle and knew she had been crying for a length of time.

"What time is your appointment?" he asked.

"At three-thirty," she said.

"All right, Granny. You get ready, and I'll be by for you at two-thirty. Will that be okay?"

"Oh, yes. Thank you. Thank you, Pastor. I'll make you a pie sometime."

"You don't have to do that, Granny, but I won't try to stop you. Everyone says you are the best cook in the church." He was happy to hear her soft laughter.

After Granny Hansley hung up, Scott arose and went into the outer office to tell his secretary the problem; he knew her concern.

It was three o'clock when Scott and Granny Hansley arrived in Cantrell. As he had thought it would be, the 30-minute trip had been fun for him. The perky, little Mrs. Hansley, free from her tears and worry, kept him entertained with tales of her early life in the Appalachian Mountains and her stay as a teacher in Alaska for five years.

Because of Granny's insistence, he asked the receptionist how long Mrs. Hansley's appointment would take. When he was assured that she would be there until five o'clock, he consented to Granny's insistence that he leave and browse around town. He really did want to go to the book store.

He had seen a Books-a-Million when they first came into town. He reasoned he could go there, get the book he wanted, and splurge on an expensive cup of coffee. He walked to the corner to use the crossing lines. Before entering the store, he picked up a newspaper from the stand outside the entrance. He tucked it under his arm and began browsing. He already knew the title he wanted, but he could never go into a book store without scanning many books. He had loved reading since grammar school days.

Although he was enjoying himself, he kept checking his watch. He didn't want to keep Granny waiting. He selected the volume he wanted, paid for it, and went to the coffee section. Once he had his mug of foamy expresso, he chose a corner seat and spread out his newspaper. He was sipping and reading when suddenly he stopped. There at the top of the feature page was a huge, colored picture of Judith Johnson. She wore a quaint blue dress with a tight bodice and knee-length gathered skirt. Her shining hair hung in two long braids as she stood, leaning slightly backward, facing a handsome young man who was firmly holding her hands. Both were smiling.

Scott had a sinking feeling before he began reading the story. He was somewhat relieved, however, to learn that the picture was a promotion for a play that was to be given at Cantrell's Community Theater. Judith Johnson and Robert Street had the leading roles. Noting the show dates, he realized that the first of two-night performances was scheduled for the upcoming Friday Quickly, he removed the little notebook he carried inside his jacket and checked to see if he had anything that he must do at that time. He was pleased to see that Friday and Saturday evenings were free. He could come to both performances; unfortunately, he knew he could not attend the Sunday matinee.

He finished his coffee and hurried to the car. He left the paper turned to the play write-up. As he headed back to the doctor's office, he kept glancing down. *So, Judith, this is what you have been doing. I'm sure you haven't given me another thought.* But how could that be? He could still see her sitting across from him, her eyes filled with tears as you told him about the death of her father. It was then that he had reached over and covered her folded hands. Their eyes had met; and with that touch, he had felt as though an electrical charge had passed between them. He remembered thinking about his college roommate who always judged poor dates by saying, "There just wasn't any electricity there." He had thought that a stupid statement; but, at that moment, he understood what Joe had meant.

Once he had seated Granny beside him in the car, he handed her the paper and said. "Look, Granny Hansley. That's the girl I'm going to marry."

Granny squinted and held the paper closer. "Well, Son, I think you have a problem. That young guy is holding on to her, and I don't like the look in his eyes."

"I know," Scott said. "I've got to do something about that. Do you have any suggestions?"

For the rest of the trip home, Scott told Granny about his chance meeting with Judith and listened as the wise little lady gave him advice. He smiled, thinking Granny's need for a ride to Cantrell was probably God's way of providing a confidant when he needed one.

"Now, Pastor, I don't mean to be bossy, but I think you should buy some new clothes before you call on that young lady. You need something different from those conservative black and gray suits you usually wear. You need to snaz things up a bit."

Scott laughed, then asked, "Do you really think so?"

"Absolutely, Son. It looks as though you might have some competition and you had better get prepared."

"What would you suggest, dear lady?" Scott said as he tilted his head and smiled.

"Well, I think you ought to buy a sports jacket and some sharp slacks. Let's see. Why not a navy blue blazer and gray pants? Oh, yes, and some black loafers!"

"Now, how do you know what young men are wearing?" Scott asked, surprised at Granny's specifics.

"I may be old, but I look at those handsome models in the magazines, and I know what they're wearing."

They had reached Granny's driveway. Scott hurried to open the door and to escort his cherished, little friend to the front door. He stooped and kissed the top of her head.

He was still smiling as he backed from the drive and headed for Zilford's leading men's store.

Friday evening Scott stood before the mirror, looking at his new image. It was true. The more casual look was better for the occasion. He wondered if Judith would remember how he was dressed before. He wondered if she would even remember him. He prayed as he left the house, *Lord, I don't know why this girl has such a hold on me, but I cannot get her out of my mind. If she is the one you have picked out for me, please, work things out for us. Help her to feel about me the way I feel about her."*

Thirty minutes later, he entered the theater and requested to be seated about mid-way back in the center section. Somehow he hoped Judith would not spot him in the audience. He remembered in college how the students would peek from behind the curtains to spot family members and friends. He wondered if this cast was doing the same thing now. To avoid being seen, he slumped behind the tall man who sat in front of him, planning to straighten up later to enjoy the performance. He would see Judith afterwards.

The play went off without flaws. No forgotten lines No scenery disasters (even though he didn't expect any scenery problems since he remembered *Our Town* had very few props). No misinterpreted lines. Scott was surprised at the professionalism of the actors and actresses. He honored the director.

During the intermission, he slipped from the auditorium and waited in the hallway until it was time for the final curtains He really wanted to surprise Judith.

The play ended with thunderous applause, Scott being one of the loudest clappers.

The cast took several curtain calls with the Stage Manager George, and Emily being the last to take their bows.

Judith was radiant, especially when someone came on stage and presented her a white tissue-wrapped bouquet of long-stemmed red roses. Smiling, she lifted her hand and blew kisses to the crowd.

Gradually, the applause subsided and the audience began filing out. Except when he stood to let someone by, Scott sat in his seat. Many people were lingering, waiting to go onto the stage to congratulate various actors and actresses. Scott watched, reveling in the excitement. Reveling, that is, until he saw the "George" character draw Judith into his arms for a warm hug. She laughed happily and did not pull away. Almost instantly the Stage Manager raced across the stage and lifted Judith up and swung her around. In spite of the aged makeup, Scott could tell the Stage Manager was really a young man, a young man who seemed far too interested in Emily. Scott's heart sank as Judith responded to his swirl with a merry giggle, a giggle that had attracted him the first time he saw her.

Without waiting longer, Scott left without speaking to Judith.

Chapter 6

Saturday morning Scott arose very early and went to the church. He liked Saturdays when all staff members were gone and he could study and meditate alone. Once, while he was in seminary, he had met an outstanding minister who each Saturday had walked up and down the aisles of his sanctuary, praying for those who would sit on the pews the next day. This was a practice Scott had followed since the first week he began his pastorate at the Community Church. Praying for his people made him feel close to them.

After his walk around the auditorium, he took a front seat and began his talk with the Lord. "Father," he said, "I'm here again. I have a special need that I want to present to you. You know that several weeks ago I met the girl I thought you had picked to be my wife. I still would like to marry Judith Johnson, but I do not know if that is possible. It seems there are other people in her life. Now, here's my problem. Judith will be in a play tonight, and I need you to tell me whether I should go to the performance. My sermons are complete and I already have a ticket. Will you, please, give me leadership."

When he began to dress that evening, Scott looked at his new coat and slacks. Judith had not seen him the night before; so he decided to wear this Granny-inspired attire again. This evening he would definitely speak to Judith. He would see if she remembered him.

As he had done on Friday evening, he entered the theater late and sought to be unobtrusive. Unfortunately, there was no tall person seated in front of him; hence he was forced to lower his head and pretend to be reading his program until the lights went down.

The play was even better the second night. Every actor was at his very best; scenery changes were made without a hitch; and the story was heart reaching. Scott felt sadness when Emily died. He thought of the great loss to the world if the bright, happy Judith Johnson were to depart.

After the curtain calls, the entire cast was scheduled to form a receiving line in the foyer. Scott planned to move through the line with everyone else, anticipating speaking with only one person – Emily.

From his place in line, he could see Judith, but she could not see him. He became disturbed when he noted the lineup – the Stage Manager, Emily, and George standing close to each other. Often he saw one or the other of the young men touch Emily's arm or hand.

Seemingly, she relished their attention.

Again, Scott slipped from the Community Theater without speaking to the cast.

Sunday morning before showering, Scott went to the closet to choose his clothes. The rack was filled with stylish suits - all solid black, navy blue, or dark gray - and several freshly laundered shirts – all white. His newly-bought clothes, quite different, drew his attention. He reasoned that he had worn the new matched jacket and slacks two evenings in a row, but no one in his church had ever seen him dressed in such casual clothing. He would see if they even noticed.

They noticed right away. "Oh, honey," Mrs. Britton said to her husband in Scott's presence, "doesn't our pastor look sharp today!"

"I'll say!" Mr. Britton said, tapping Scott's shoulder.

Two teenaged girls snickered as they complemented him, and the Jolson boys gave him a thumbs-up gesture. Others voiced their approval, causing the surprised pastor to smile. *Whoever said, "Clothes make a man" must have known something. I think I might need to go back to Zilford's Clothing Store. Judith might like the new me.*

After he had stood in the foyer, greeting everyone before Sunday school and before church, Scott returned to his study. As his custom was, he opened his Bible to read the verse he always read before going to his pulpit. He had just turned the pages to I Timothy 1:12 which thanked the Lord for putting him into the ministry when, suddenly, there was an unexpected rap on his door.

"Come in," Scott called politely.

The door opened and the stalwart Dr. Gilham entered the room. Scott rose to his feet, ready to have his morning's elation deflated. He was surprised, however, when the deacon spoke.

"Pastor," Dr. Gilham began. (Dr. Gilham had never called him Pastor.) "I need to ask a favor of you." (Scott was shocked.)

"What can I do for you?" the pastor asked.

"Pastor, you know I have a son, Michael, Jr., who was graduated first in his class at Harvard." Scott nodded. (Everyone in the church had heard this boast many times.) "Yes?" Scott said, realizing that it was almost time for him to head to the sanctuary. He placed his notes inside his Bible and edged toward the door, respectfully keeping his eyes focused on Dr. Gilham. A stickler for starting all services on time, he knew he had only minutes to spare.

"My son is here today." Dr. Gilham began. "He came to honor his mother's birthday; but I need you to know that since he was twenty years old, Michael has claimed to be an atheist. His mother and I have never wanted anyone to know this. We've not been able to understand. You see, when he was a child, we brought him to church regularly. In his adult life, however, he has blatantly belittled Christianity. In fact, today will be the first day he has been in church since he went away to college."

"I'm sincerely sorry to hear that," Scott said with compassion. "Is there anything I can do?"

"Yes. That's why I'm here. Could you, please, speak on, eh, on a higher level so that you would be more apt to reach him? So far, no one has ever been able to reason with him on his plain."

For the first time, Dr. Gilham noted the blue blazer and the gray slacks and wished the pastor had been wearing the more distinguished black.

"On a different level?" Scott was puzzled.

Words tumbled from Dr. Gilham's mouth as though rehearsed. Gone was his haughty demeanor. "Well," he said, "I mean could you cease being so conversational…you know…could you use a more ministerial tone ….you know what I mean…. and drop…. you know, Pastor, you have a good sense of humor, but could you drop that today?" He took a deep breath and continued, "And one other thing: could you, please, preach on some non-threatening topic? My wife and I would appreciate it so very much if you would do these things for us. We may never get Michael in church again."

Scott looked directly into Dr. Gilham's eyes, "Dr. Gilham," he said, "I've spent hours on my message. I really believe it is what the Lord wants me to preach. Now, if the Lord has laid this message on my heart, surely he can use it to speak to your son. I hope you understand; I cannot change what I know I must preach."

Dr. Gilham heaved a defeated sigh; and for the first time, Scott noted humility in this usually arrogant man.

"Sir," Scott said with compassion, "let's pray for your son right now and we'll leave the rest to the Lord." He bent slightly and placed his placed his right hand on Dr. Gilham's shoulder..

Dr. Gilham eased closer and bowed his head. The two prayed.

Most of the members of the Zilford Community Church had left by 12:30, but the Gilman Family and close friends lingered, tearfully embracing each other. Michael Gilham, Jr., had awed everyone when he was the first person to respond to the pastor's invitation at the end of the morning sermon. The young minister had knelt by Michael, speaking with him quietly and pointing to various Scripture verses. At length, he placed his arm over Michael's shoulders and prayed.

When the two men stood, Michael asked to speak.

For the next ten minutes he explained what had happened to him his freshman year in college. He had taken a psychology class under a brilliant, atheistic teacher with whom he formed a friendship. Day by day, this intellectual professor had discredited everything Michael had ever been taught. Later, this imposing mentor invited him to meet with a group of young scholars who held similar beliefs. Here friendships were forged, causing Michael to separate himself completely from Christianity.

Now, he turned and apologized to his father and mother for the way he had ridiculed their attempts to rekindle his faith. He admitted that even when he was adamant about his beliefs, offering arguments he knew his parents could not debate, deep within he had secretly wished he could once again believe as they did.

"When your pastor preached his sermon this morning, 'What shall it profit a man if he gain the whole world and lose his own soul,' it was as though the truth I held when I was a child flooded my life again."

Unchecked tears wet his cheeks as he admitted that he had been busy coveting a high status in life while his soul was starving. He finished speaking and turned to shake the pastor's hand, warmly covering their clasped hands with his left hand. Then, instinctively, he exchanged the firm handshake for an appreciative hug.

Onlookers cried. Dr. Gilham extended his hand to Pastor Jacobs, then wrapped his arms around the young minister, patting his back fatherly.

"Thank the Lord for you, Pastor. Thank the Lord for you."

Chapter 7

As the teachers sat in the lounge Monday morning, Elaine Manix spoke to Judith. "Say, Judith, didn't you say you met the preacher of Zilford's Community Church?"

"Yes. Why?" Judith said.

"Oh, noting except he attended both Friday and Saturday evening performances. I know because I took his ticket."

Judith's heart seemingly skipped a beat. "Really? Are you sure?" Her heart beat faster

"Of course, I'm sure. My aunt attends that church and I've visited with her several times. I wonder why Pastor Jacobs came to see the play twice. Did he speak to you?"

"No. I didn't know he was there," Judith answered, trying to sound unconcerned.

"I had hoped to talk with him after the performance, but he must have slipped by while I was talking with someone else," Elaine continued. "He is usually very friendly. I'm surprised that he did not, at least, go through the line to speak to you."

He probably doesn't even remember me," she said.

"I bet he does. He has a knack for remembering names of everyone he meets. That is one of his strong points, according to my aunt."

Judith said nothing else, for she was busy thinking about

Friday and Saturday evenings. Did Scott Jacobs see Robert and Zack hugging her? Did he misunderstand? Could he possibly care? *Dear Lord, help him to understand their hugs meant nothing. Nothing at all.*

Back in class, Judith sought to teach "noun clauses" in an interesting way, but her thoughts kept reverting to the lounge conversation. Nagging thoughts tormented her. She scolded herself. Why couldn't she get Scott Jacobs out of her mind?

A week later, Judith approached Elaine in the hallway and said nonchalantly, "You know, Elaine, I would like to go to church with you and your aunt someday. I've heard that Community Church is the most outstanding church in our area. I really would like to attend sometime." She hoped Elaine would not think she wanted to see Scott. It surprised her that she no longer thought of the minister as Scott Jacobs; often now in her mind and prayers she called him Scott.

If the connection with Pastor Jacobs crossed Elaine's mind, she did not mention it. She smiled and said, "Oh, I know that would make Aunt Miriam very happy. She thinks her church is the greatest church in the world and declares her pastor is the best preacher she has ever heard."

"Well, you have heard him preach. What do you think?"

"I think I have to agree with my aunt. Pastor Jacobs is superb. I really would like for you to hear him. When do you want to go?"

"I am free this Sunday if that would fit your plans. Mother has gone to Nashville to visit her sister, and this weekend would be a good time for me."

"Good. I'll call Aunt Miriam to tell her to expect us. I know she will want us to eat lunch with her. Will that be all right?"

"Yes, that would be great. I know the cookies she has baked for the teacher's lounge have been delicious, and I've heard you brag about her meals."

Judith felt foolish and somewhat guilty about the small talk; however, she walked into her classroom, relieved that the plan had been made. She was to meet Elaine and her aunt at church Sunday morning at 10:45. She was the one who had suggested the time, for she did not want to get there too early. Hopefully, Scott would not see her until she shook hands with him at the door.

Seemingly, the week dragged by. The play was over. Her mother was away. On purpose, she avoided Zack at school and failed to return Mike's calls. She was merely counting the days until she could go to Community Church.

Saturday morning she checked through her wardrobe. Nothing appealed to her. She wondered why women forever fretted over clothes. She would bet that Scott had five or six conservative suits, hangers of starched shirts, and a collection of blue and maroon ties. He probably could go into his closet, in the dark, and pick out a suitable combination. On the other hand she, a woman, had to consider the fashion trends of the day, the current popular fabrics, and the appropriate outfit for each occasion. How foolish.

At length, she settled on a soft pink, woolen dress. She mused she would hate for anyone to know what had determined her choice. Even though she knew that pastel pinks, yellows, and blues were her best colors, she had really chosen pink because of something she had read recently. The article had stated that pink is the color that attracts men the most. It wasn't, exactly, that she wanted to attract Scott, but she did want to look her best when she saw him again. Would it even matter? What if he did not remember her? It had been months since they first met.

When Judith walked up the church steps, Elaine said, "My. My. Don't you look stunning! That must be your Sunday dress; I've never seen you wear it to school."

Judith laughed. "All country girls save their best clothes for Sunday, didn't you know?"

"But you're no country girl," Elaine said and turned to her aunt. "Aunt Miriam, this is my fellow teacher, Judith Johnson. Judith pretended she wanted to come to church, but I believe she just wanted to eat one of your great meals. Like me, she lives alone and does not do much cooking."

"Well, we'll see what we can do about that, but we had better get inside. We may have to sit near the back. Our sanctuary fills up quickly."

"Oh, that would suit me fine," Judith said. "I may get to coughing and have to get up to leave. If I am nearer the back, I will not disturb so much." *Not exactly a lie. I do have a scratchy throat,* Judith thought.

Aunt Miriam was right; already there was little room left. An usher led them to a seat in the center several rows from the back. Judith was grateful to sit behind a woman wearing a wide-brimmed hat.

Judith noticed a happy buzz of voices and titters of laughter, something her church did not have. Her sanctuary was reverently quiet. She looked around. The people seemed happy, relaxed. She, too, felt a sense of ease.

The organist began to play, and an immediate silence fell. Those who had been greeting friends took their seats. It was as though the whole congregation was filled with expectation. She could understand why when two side doors opened and a choir of 40 or 50 marched to their places, wearing blue robes and cream-colored stoles.

Scott Jacobs came through another door and walked up to the pulpit. Judith's heart beat faster, but she wanted to smile. Scott was wearing a blue suit, a white shirt, and a maroon tie.

"Choir members do not take your seats," he said. Turning back to the audience, he said, "You folks know that in the past I was not too keen on robes, but our choir wanted them so that they could all look alike. Now, I must say I am well pleased. Don't they look grand!" Applause erupted. Applause in church. Another first for Judith.

"You may be seated," he said to the choir and, "thank you." He walked to the podium and said, "I have another great treat today. My parents, my two brothers, and my sister are here today. They arrived this morning as a surprise. Mom, Dad and you other guys, will you, please, stand so that my people may see the major influences in my life."

The Jacobs Family stood, slightly turned, and smiled. Judith peeked around the big hat. She wanted to know Scott's family. What a perfect day she had chosen to visit the Zilford Community Church. She might be able to speak to them.

All normal procedures – the welcoming of visitors, the offertory, the congregational singing: all meshed together with heartfelt enthusiasm. With perfection, the choir sang a medley of Christian hymns, ending with "Amazing Grace." Judith enjoyed every aspect of the service; but, for a moment, she held her breath when the choir had descended into the audience and Scott went to the pulpit to preach.

For his text he chose the New Testament's best-known verse of scripture, the first verse she had memorized in Sunday School. Hearing the rustling of Bible leaves, she was glad she had brought her Bible. She turned to John 3:16 and followed the words as Scott read aloud, *"For God so loved the world that he gave his only begotten son that whosoever believeth on him should not perish but have everlasting life."*

Considering that this verse was probably the most familiar one he could have chosen, Judith wondered how Scott could preach for 30 minutes or more, saying anything that was new or thought provoking. From his introduction to the final conclusion, however, Scott Jacobs preached the greatest sermon that Judith had ever heard. Tears ran down her cheeks as several people responded to an invitation at the conclusion of the message.

Judith dabbed around her eyes, hoping that her brown eyeliners would not smudge.

Before Scott could pronounce the benediction, suddenly Dr. Gilham arose and said, "Just a minute, Pastor Jacobs. I have something to say."

Judith stared at Scott for the blood, seemingly, drained from his face. Dr. Gilham mounted the steps to the platform, having a rolled up sheet of paper in his hand. "We need to handle a matter now," he said. Scott had stepped aside as Dr. Gilham strode to the pulpit. His heart pounded. He had thought that everything was right between Dr. Gilham and himself since Michael.... but now......

Before Dr. Gilham could speak, a noise drew the attention of the congregation. All eyes turned as a side door banged open and grinning 12-year-old Philip Peterson came forward, bearing a huge triple-layered cake glowing with 27 white candles. Dr. Gilham began singing, "Happy Birthday"; and, as on cue, the congregation chimed in heartily.

"Pastor, we had a hard time keeping this from you. We learned from the Petersons that you have a birthday coming up Tuesday. Now, since the Peterson family has spearheaded this surprise, I am going to ask Brother Peterson to come up. I think he has a few things he would like to say."

Beaming, Mr. Peterson came to the platform, embraced the pastor, and patted him on the back. Again there was applause. Mr. Peterson stepped to the pulpit.

"Pastor, you have been with us almost two years, and we thought it was time for us to celebrate your birthday. Until last week, we did not know your birth date. Fortunately, we learned by the grapevine. Now, I hope you don't mind; but during the church service, a catered meal has been set up in the fellowship room. You and your family will be our guests of honor, but we want everyone to stay for lunch. Will that be all right with you?"

"All right? Of course it will be all right. I would never want anyone to miss this wonderful thing you have done for me. Thank you, everyone." He shook his head in humble, but happy, astonishment.

Judith felt as though her heart would burst. She had never been so very happy. She loved Scott Jacobs. She loved his church. His people.

Mr. Peterson took over again. "And now, Pastor, I have asked Debbie to come to escort you to the fellowship hall.

Judith was amazed to see a beautiful young girl glide up to Scott's side and hook her arm into his. She flipped her long black hair over her shoulder; and, smiling up at him, led him from the room. In dismay, Judith noted that she was wearing a frosty pink dress that accented her loveliness.

Judith could not stay for the meal, not with Scott and his gorgeous escort clad in the softest, frosty pink dress she had ever seen. She scolded herself. She should have known that the handsome Scott Jacobs, with his flirtatious charm, would have a girlfriend. Thankful that she had driven her car, Judith feigned a headache and slipped hurriedly away.

When Judith entered her apartment, she flipped on her answering machine. As she expected, there was a message from Zack. She was surprised, however, that there was also a message from Robert Street. She had heard from Robert only twice since he and she had been George and Emily in "Our Town." Once he had asked her to go to dinner with him and another time, to go with him to a concert; each time she had declined. If he called again, she reasoned, it would be good for her to accept any kind of invitation. It was time for her to forget Scott Jacobs.

Robert called later that evening and asked her to attend a college banquet with him. This time she said, "I would be delighted to go with you." Strangely, she meant it.

Chapter 8

Once again, Scott had taken Granny Hansley to Cantrell for a doctor's appointment and once again she had insisted that he must not sit idly in the waiting room. She encouraged him to go for a walk or to get something to eat. With a grin, she added, "Or sit on a bench and watch the pretty girls go by."

Scott chuckled as he left the building. He knew Granny and her husband must have had a great marriage. He loved her sense of humor.

It was May, and Mother's Day was only a week away. He had not yet bought his mother a card; so he headed for the Hallmark Card Shop. When he entered the decorated entrance, he experienced a warm sensation, not because of the merry tinkle of the doorbell and not because of the colorful display of cardboard life-like mothers holding children in their arms. No, the sensation he felt was far more personal. It was here he had first met Judith Johnson.

A lovely middle-aged clerk greeted him warmly. "May I help you?" she asked.

"Well, yes. I am here to get a Mother's Day card. Maybe you could point me in the right direction."

The lovely lady responded to his smile. "Go down the center aisle. The Mother's Day cards will be on your left."

He had barely said, "Thank you" and walked away when the clerk whispered to another clerk. "Look. That's the young man who asked a young girl to marry him in the store last fall, remember?"

"I remember," the second clerk responded, "and do you know what? I believe that same girl is in the card section now."

Both ladies left their posts and, unobtrusively, eased nearer the Mother's Day display.

Scott stopped. He had not dared to hope that Judith would once again be in the card section, but there she stood, her blonde hair gleaming under the bright overhead lights. She had lifted a card to read when he stepped up behind her and said, "Pick out one for me, too, please." Shocked, she dropped the card back into its slot.

Her hair slipped over her shoulder as she turned quickly to look up into the face she had seen in her mind a thousand times.

"Oh, Scott Jacobs!" she exclaimed. *You idiot*, she chided herself. *You have let him know you remembered his name, his full name at that!*

"Hello, Judith," Scott said and then added three drawn-out words. "I've missed you."

"I've missed you, too," she whispered and then immediately scolded herself. Why did she always blurt out her innermost thoughts when she was near this man!

Mindful of no one else, only the beautiful girl who stood before him, Scott reached down and drew her two hands to his chest.

"Do you remember that once, in this very spot, I asked you to marry me?"

"I remember," Judith said breathlessly with a slight nod.

"Well, I'm going to ask you again today and I want you to say, 'Yes.'" Still holding her hands, he stepped arms-length away.

He looked intently into Judith's eyes. "Judith Johnson, will you marry me? I want you to be my wife. Will you marry me?"

When she hesitated, he said, "I'll get down on one knee if that is the way you want me to propose."

"Oh, no. That will not be necessary," Judith said with her musical laugh that he treasured.

"Well, will you marry me?

"Scott, we hardly know each other. You haven't even met my mother."

"I saw her at the play. She's beautiful, just an older replica of you. I know I'll love her. And, don't worry about my family. We are all like peas in a pod. If you care for me, you'll love the whole Jacobs Clan." Judith could only look into his eyes and smile.

"Well," Scott said rather loudly with a downward tilt of his head. "Will you marry me?"

"Yes," Judith whispered as tears filled her eyes.

Suddenly, the two were surrounded by applause. Surprised, Scott and Judith glanced around to see that several people had encircled them. One small gray-haired man peered over the rim of his glasses and said, "She said 'Yes,' Sonny Boy. Kiss her!"

Scott laughed. "I believe I will." He drew Judith into his arms and kissed her for the first time. It was a sweet, soft, lingering kiss. When he released her, snickers and applause signified approval.

"Thank you," Scott said, grinning. "You're all invited to our wedding. Since we do not know you, we will not be able to send you an invitation; but you can watch for our announcement in the paper. My name is Rev. Scott Jacobs and this is your local teacher, Judith Johnson."

Judith stood speechless with her hand over her heart. *Can this be happening? Did I just consent to marry Scott Jacobs?*

"I need a Mother's Day card," she whispered. A thoughtful

clerk stepped forward and pointed out, what she called "the prettiest card in the house."

"I need another just like that one," Scott said, reaching for his billfold. As the clerk led the way to the cash register, Scott and Judith followed, stopping to shake hands with several who wished them happiness.

The small gray-headed gentleman added, "May the Lord bless you and keep you." Scott thought he would have quoted the whole benediction had he not been interrupted by a little old lady who wanted to say something. She patted Scott's arm and said, "You two are going to have pretty children. Son, you are just about the most handsome young man I have ever seen and you, my dear," she said turning to Judith, "are as purty as a picture."

As soon as they had left the store, Scott grinned. "I believe they would have thrown rice on us if they'd had it." Holding hands, they laughed as they crossed the street.

"Leave your car here for now," Scott said, "I have someone I want you to meet."

Judith surprised him by saying, "Wherever you go, I will go. Your people will be my people. Your God, my God."

Scott knew Granny would love Judith.

Scott was right. Granny did love Judith. The three ate supper in a quaint little cafeteria that specialized in home-style food with a soft-music atmosphere that encouraged conversation. As the two women talked, Scott realized that Judith was responding to Granny's wit with her own witticism. It was as though they had always known each other.

"You must come to our church," Granny said, "so that Pastor can introduce you to our church family. Everyone will be so happy that he's getting married. It has kept the women in our church busy trying to cook for him. By the way, you can cook, can't you?"

"Well, yes. A little. What I don't know, you can teach me."

"I'll do that. But now, we'd better get going. My little dog will be worried about me."

As they walked to the car, Scott said, "You know, I think Granny is right. I need to have you with me when I announce we're going to get married." Suddenly, he thought of Dr. Gilham and the threat he had once made. Would he remember the first time he saw Judith and his harsh comments? Would he now be able to accept her? Would he, in reality, be relieved that his bachelor pastor was getting married? He wondered if he should talk with Dr. Gilham before he made the announcement. Although he was really concerned about Dr. Gilham's reaction, he knew the rest of his congregation would be pleased.

Chapter 9

J udith hurried into her mother's home. "Mom! Mom!" she called excitedly.

Mrs. Johnson ran from the kitchen. "What? What, Judith? Is something wrong?"

Judith grabbed her mother and twirled her around. "No... no....no. Everything is perfect. I'm going to get married! I'm going to get married!"

Her mother pushed away slightly. "Married? But I didn't think you really cared for Zack or Mike or even Robert."

"I don't. It's not one of them. I am going to marry the preacher of the Zilford Community Church."

"Are you serious? Are you talking about the young man who asked you to marry him the first time you met?"

"Yes. Yes. Yes, the very same one!"

"Let me sit down. I go off for one week and I come back to find that my daughter is going to get married.....and.....to someone I have never met."

"Oh, but, Mother, you will love him. Everyone does."

Judith sat down on the floor beside her mother's chair and detailed the wonderful things that had been happening. For an hour, Mrs. Johnson sat with her hands folded in her lap, reveling in her daughter's happiness.

"Now, Mother," Judith said. "Scott is going to tell his church the news Sunday, and he wants us to be there."

"Oh, dear me," Mrs. Johnson sighed. "Everything is happening so very fast."

"Look, Mother, I am 24 years old. I want to get married. I want to start a family. You do want grandchildren, don't you?"

"Of course I want grandchildren, Judith. And you are right. If you have found a young man you love, you should marry." She stood. "Would you like to go up into the attic to see my wedding gown I have saved for you all these years?"

With their arms wrapped around each other, they headed for the attic stairs.

Scott had never been happier in his life. He could hardly wait to call his parents. *I'm afraid they thought I would never get married. Wait until I tell them about Judith. They will love her. Now, I have to do this right.* His thoughts were wild.. *I want to tell both of them at the same time.* He dialed the number and tried to calm himself down by taking two deep breaths.

"Mom, get Dad on the other phone! I have something to tell both of you. Hurry."

He could hear his mother calling, and then there was a click. "Hi Son, what's up?"

"I'm getting married! I've found the girl the Lord has for me!"

"Married?" his mother whispered, "But we didn't know you were going with anyone."

"I haven't exactly been going with her, but I have loved her since the first time we met. She's a high school teacher. She's wonderful. You will love her."

"Hold on, Son," his dad said. "What does your church think about this sudden decision?"

"I haven't told them yet, but I know they will be pleased. The women are always feeling sorry for me living by myself.

They think they have to bring me casseroles and desserts every week, and they are forever telling me I need a good wife. And you know what, Dad? I agree with them."

"When are you planning to tell your people?" his dad said.

"Sunday morning. That is why I am calling. Could you come over to be with us? I would like for Judith to be sitting with you."

"Judith," his mother said. "Judith…that was my grandmother's name."

"Isn't that strange? That was her great grandmother's name, too."

"Son," Mrs. Jacobs said, "You know your grandmother wanted me to save her rings for your bride someday. Do you want me to bring them, or have you already bought rings?"

"No, Mom, I haven't bought anything. I always planned to use Grandmother's rings. They are beautiful and I'm sure Judy will love them, Please bring them."

Mr. Jacobs broke in. "Okay, Son. I've just looked at my calendar. I believe we can make it this weekend. We'll come on Saturday; now, I suppose we should meet our future daughter-in-law even before we go to church together. Prepare your sermons early so that we can go out for dinner Saturday evening. Choose your best restaurant and make reservations for us. The treat will be on me."

"Thanks, Dad. I'll be looking for you Saturday afternoon. We'll have a lot to talk about. Well, I had better go. I have many things to do. I love you, Mom and Dad."

Mr. and Mrs. Jacobs said their customary love yous, hung up, and met in the hallway to hug each other. Their prayers were being answered.

Only Granny Hansley knew about the Pastor's plans. Because of his closeness to the Petersons, however, Scott felt he should tell them; but when he reached their home Friday afternoon, he learned from neighbors that the Petersons had gone shopping in Charlotte and would not be back until late Saturday. He started to leave a note; but then, considered he could not do this important message justice in just a few words. He would simply have to wait to share the good news with his closest friends, the Petersons, Sunday morning before church. He knew they would rejoice with him. Only a week ago, Mr. Peterson had winked at him and said, "What you need, Pastor, is a good wife."

Sunday morning dawned a perfect spring day. No cold cereal for breakfast. His mother had fried bacon, scrambled eggs, and baked her famous, homemade biscuits. Scott ate and left early, planning to walk prayerfully through the sanctuary and then to go over his notes one last time. Even though he had thoroughly prepared, he feared he might be up tight, considering the big announcement he was to make at the end of the service.

Usually, his Sunday morning message claimed his undivided attention. Today, however, he could not control his thoughts. His mind kept envisioning the beautiful Judith Johnson standing by his side as he introduced her as his bride-to-be. He imagined the congregation's applause and, maybe, a standing ovation of warm approval.

He drove into his parking place. He smiled, glad this space had been designated with one word: PASTOR. Pastor. He liked that. He really wanted his congregation to think of him as their pastor.

He was standing in the vestibule, greeting Sunday school students when the Petersons arrived. He wanted to rush out into the parking lot to tell them the news; but one of the deacons tapped him on the arm and said, "Pastor, you are wanted on the phone."

He excused himself and went into his study.

"Pastor Jacobs speaking," he said with a lilt to his voice.

"Scott," Judith said. "Mother and I are running a little late; so we are going to ask to be seated with your parents when we arrive. Is that all right?"

"Of course, Honey. I hope nothing is wrong."

"Oh, no. Mother just spilled coffee on her dress and is having to change. She's as nervous as I am." Her soft laughter warmed his heart.

"OK, Judith, I'll tell Mom and Dad to save you a place. Be praying for me. I might need help getting through things this morning."

"You'll be great. I can hardly wait for Mother to hear you preach. Bye now."

When Scott hurried back into the foyer, he noted the Sunday school superintendent leading Mr. Peterson down the hall, explaining a need as they walked. "One of Doctor Markham's patients has gone into labor and he can't teach this morning. He asked me to have you teach. I hope you are prepared, Brother."

"Well, you can rest assured I have studied. Since I'm the assistant for an obstetrician, I always try to be prepared. This will not be the first time I've taught with a moment's notice. But, you know me; I like to teach."

From the time the choir marched in with their new robes and Scott came from the side entrance, the morning service was superb. The congregation laughed when the pastor made announcements and reported that a first grader asked him earlier that morning if he used to play with Abraham Lincoln. The choir's rendition of an arrangement of "When We All Get to Heaven" led fittingly into Scott's message, a message on heaven, a message he preached with great liberty. Everything was perfect.

The service ended; but instead of the benediction, Scott asked everyone to be seated. Then he called for Judith Johnson to come to the platform. Smiling and trying hard to keep from trembling, Judith held her Bible close to her chest as she eased from the pew and mounted the red carpeted steps.

When she was by his side, Scott said, "You people know that I love you with all my heart. You have treated me royally; yet, I must admit, something has been missing from my life. For the past year, I have been praying that the Lord would give me a wife. Today, I am happy to tell you that God has answered my prayers. I would like for you to meet Judith Johnson, a high school teacher from Cantrell. I've known Judith for a while now and I have asked her to marry me; and, believe it or not, she has said, 'Yes.'"

In his mind, he had expected an ovation, but he thought he heard a shocked gasp followed by an eerie hush. The silence was awkward until Granny Hansley stood and began clapping. Others joined in, some reluctantly, Scott noted. He could not understand.

Judith stood by Scott at the congregation filed out. Many congratulated the pastor and wished Judith happiness, but not with great enthusiasm. Some parishioners exited from side doors, saying nothing. Something was wrong and Scott knew it, but he tried to smooth things over as his family left for the restaurant. "I guess my surprise announcement was a little hard for them to grasp. You know, they had never seen me dating anyone."

Mr. Jacobs laughed. "I understand, Son. It was a little shocking for your mother and me." He turned to Judith and added quickly. "Not that we were not pleased, Judith. It is just that he kept you a secret from us."

Judith touched Mrs. Jacob's arm. "Someday we will explain to you. Our courtship has been quite unusual, but both of us believe it was God ordained."

"And that is all that matters, Mr. Jacobs said,

Once they were back home, Scott slipped into his bedroom to call Mr. Peterson to see why the congregation had acted as they did.

"Mr. Peterson," he said. "I need to talk with you. Something was not right this morning. Can you tell me what was wrong?"

"Yes," Mr. Peterson said curtly. "What you did today was despicable."

"Despicable?"

"Yes, despicable," Mr. Peterson said and hung up.

When Scott went back into the living room, no one had to ask if there was something wrong. The color had drained from his face. His hands were shaking.

Slipping on his suit coat, he said, "Folks, I hope you will excuse me. I have to make a call right now. Right now. I shouldn't be gone long."

No one asked questions.

Walking up the curved walkway to the Peterson's house, Scott saw the curtains move. Strange. Ominous. Before he could ring the doorbell, the door opened and Mr. Peterson stepped outside, closing the door behind him.

With a controlled voice, Mr. Peterson said, "Pastor, I'm sorry for the word 'despicable.' I hope you will forgive me. I was very upset when you called. I was upset with you."

"With me? Why?" Scott asked. "What did I do?"

"What did you do? You really don't know, do you?

"No, Sir, I don't."

"Well, I'll tell you. You broke my daughter's heart. Debbie has been crying for hours. She thought you loved her. The whole church did. Why, just this week, Mrs. Brown asked her if you two were waiting for her to be graduated before getting married."

Scott walked across the porch and sank down on the top step. He put his head into his hands. "Oh dear Lord, what have I done?" He looked up. "Mr. Peterson, believe me, I never knew Debbie felt that way about me. I am over five years older than she is, and I always thought of her as my little sister. Sir, you've seen my sister. You know how much they look alike. I told her that over and over."

"But you came to our home each Sunday, and you must have noticed that Debbie came home from college every weekend."

"I thought being with all of you was a family thing. I didn't think Debbie was coming home to see me." He stood to his feet. "Mr. Peterson, I've never kissed your daughter or even held her hand. I'm so very sorry if she thought I was leading her along. I'm sorry if I misled you. I hope you can find it in your heart to forgive me. And now, Sir, may I, please, talk with Debbie?"

"No," Mr. Peterson said. "I don't think that would be wise at this time. She is too upset. Wait. Let her go back to school. I am sure that, with what happened today, she will not come home again until after graduation. By then, maybe, she'll consent to talk with you. Do you understand?"

"Yes, Sir, if you say so; but, please, tell her how sorry I am. Tell her I do love her, but the age difference always kept me from thinking of her as anything more than my young sister. I'm so very sorry." With a heavy lump in his throat, he turned and walked away.

He did not see the curtain open and close as he headed to his car.

When Scott entered the parsonage, he found Judith and her mother seated on the sofa, talking with his parents. In a corner, his brother watched a TV ballgame with almost no sound. Scott stepped into the dining room, brought back a chair, and placed it so that he could face everyone. He motioned for his brother to turn off the television and to join them.

When all eyes were upon him, he cleared his throat and began. "I'm glad the people I love most in this world are with me right now. I've made a serious blunder, and I'm going to need your guidance....and your help."

Only Mr. Jacobs spoke. "What is it, Son? What have you done?"

"I have hurt some very dear folks. I didn't mean to, Dad. I didn't even know that I had done it. I've just found out from Mr. Peterson."

No one spoke. He continued. "I sensed something was wrong this morning, but I did not know what. Did you notice anything strange when I announced my engagement?"

In stunned silence, slowly, his listeners nodded their heads.

He looked at Judith's troubled eyes. "Honey, I'm sure this has nothing to do with my congregation approving you. You are beautiful and intelligent, everything that any minister could want in a wife....everything a church could want in a minister's wife."

Judith caught her breath. Intuitively, she knew that, somehow, she really was not Scott's problem. That was a relief.

Mr. Jacobs interrupted. "Scott, tell us what is wrong. Don't beat around the bush."

"Well, Dad, you see I just learned that Debbie Peterson thinks she's in love with me and has been counting on my marrying her. Evidently, some of the people have been encouraging her that way. I don't know why. I have never held her hand or kissed her, even on the cheek. I have never ridden alone with her in my car or taken her anywhere. I cannot understand what I did to encourage her."

"Did you ever tell her she was pretty or anything like that?" his mother asked.

"No, I don't think so. I probably told her now and then that she had on a pretty dress; but, Mom, I tell Mrs. Jones or even Granny Hansley that."

He looked again at Judith's pale face. "Judith, you know that I told you all about the Petersons and I told you how Debbie made me think of my sister."

"Yes, you told me that," Judith said, but the picture of Debbie dressed in her frosty pink dress crossed her mind. She had not liked the way the beautiful Debbie Peterson had hooked her arm into Scott's arm and led him away for his birthday party. Now, once again, she felt the slight pain she had experienced when that particular episode had happened.

After the family had discussed the matter for an hour, Judith rose. "Scott," she said, "I do not think it would be wise for me to go back to church this evening. I think Mother and I will leave now."

Scott took her two hands and placed them against his chest. "Honey, it grieves me, but I think you are right. Give this situation time, and I believe everything will be all right."

Judith tried to blink back tears. "Perhaps we should not see each other for a while." She turned to pick up her purse. "It is only three weeks before my school is out, and I will need to be very busy." She looked up into Scott's sorrowful eyes and tried to smile. "Don't worry. I'll send you an e-mail or texted messages each day, and you may call me each evening."

He drew her to him and kissed her a soft, lingering kiss that told her how much he needed her. She responded willingly, unmindful of those who filled the room.

Mrs. Jacobs broke the mood by standing and going over to hug Judith. "Bless you, child," she said. "The Lord will take care of this matter for us."

Scott looked at his father. "Dad," he said quietly, "I need some "alone time."

"I was thinking you would," Mr. Jacobs said, reaching for his jacket hanging on the chair. Mother and I need to be going anyway. We'll call later."

Scott hugged his parents goodbye; then, he went into his bedroom alone and knelt by his bed. He was glad his dad had taught him about "alone time" when he was only a little boy. Mr. Jacobs had been reading about Jesus in the Garden just before the crucifixion. At first, Jesus was with the disciples; then he took his three closest friends apart to pray. The ultimate praying happened, however, when he left the three and spent time alone with the Father. He was facing death. He was fearful. He needed this treasured "alone" time to cry out to his Father.

"Son," Mr. Jacobs had said. "There will be times when you will pray about issues in big groups. That will be fine. At other times, however, you may feel the need to ask two or three to join you in prayer; but, Son, remember, if our Savior had to have 'alone time' with the Father, many times you will need to exclude everyone so that, by yourself, you can communicate with the Father."

This was one of the times, Scott wanted to pray alone. Tears flowed freely as he poured out his troubled heart to the Father and asked for guidance.

At 5:30, he arose from his knees and, grabbing a Kleenex, headed to the bathroom where he splashed water on his face and checked to see the extent of redness in his eyes. *It will be an hour before I see anyone at church. I think I will look all right by then.* Again he prayed, *Father, help me to get through tonight's service. I need your anointing. I need your sustaining power.* He made his way to the kitchen and poured a glass of milk. He had no desire for food.

Scott was in his office, going over his evening message when the phone rang.

"Scott," Mr. Peterson said, "We will not be in church this evening. We have decided to take Debbie back to school;

however, if you have any free time tomorrow morning, I would like to come in to see you."

Scott glanced down at his calendar. "Come anytime you like," he said. "I would like to talk with you. The Lord bless you, Sir."

The evening congregation was not as large as usual, but the service went off smoothly. The choir number was great and several people responded to the invitation at the end of the sermon. Scott breathed a sigh of relief as he turned off his office light and closed the door behind him. The Lord had brought him over the first hurdle. Tomorrow he knew he would face Mr. Peterson again, but he was determined he would rely upon divine wisdom for that encounter.

Chapter 10

ven though Scott had truly sought to commit the impending meeting with Mr. Peterson to the Lord, he slept fitfully, awaking periodically with troublesome thoughts. *How could he have hurt the Peterson family – the family that had shown him the most love – the family that had encouraged him the most? What did he do to make Debbie misunderstand his feelings for her? What could he say or do now to undo the hurt?*

At five o'clock, he arose, showered, and dressed before pressing the coffee maker's "on" button, Methodically, he put two pieces of toast in the toaster and opened the refrigerator to remove the butter and jelly. He had no appetite, but he ate.

Having cleared the table, he sat with his Bible opened before him. He read again where Jesus instructed his disciples to take no thought for what they were to say when the going was rough.

"Lord," he prayed. "I need your help now. I need wisdom. Father, you know I didn't mean to hurt anyone. I didn't know I was encouraging Debbie Peterson. And now, dear Lord, I ask you to bless and guide me as I talk with Mr. Peterson." He lingered at the table, reading scriptures and praying.

At six-thirty, he drove up the driveway to Community Church. The rising sun cast a warm glow upon the rows of pink and white Dogwood trees lining the driveway, but scenery held no appeal for Scott. His mind refused to consider anything, anything other than his facing Mr. Peterson.

Mr. Peterson arrived promptly at 7 o'clock. He entered the office, seemingly as uneasy as the young pastor was. He took a seat across from Scott's desk.

"May I get you a cup of coffee?" Scott asked before he took his seat.

"No, thank you," Mr. Peterson said. "I've already had my two-cup limit."

Scott took his seat, leaned forward, folded his trembling hands upon the desk, and asked "Now, Sir, before we start our conversation, allow me once again to tell you how deeply sorry that I am that I've caused any sorrow in your home. I have loved your family as my own and would never have purposely done anything to cause you any trouble." He sat back and sighed. "Now, Brother Peterson, is there something you want to say to me? Please say whatever you need to say."

Mr. Peterson pressed his lips together and then began, "Pastor, it is true that we are experiencing some sorrow in our home at the present. As you know, we are a very close family; and when one person in our household hurts, we all hurt."

Scott lowered his eyes and nodded.

Mr. Peterson continued. "You and I have a love for the Lord, a love that will not let our personal affairs to interfere with our work here at Community Church; therefore, we must find a way to bridge our difficulties."

Again Scott nodded without speaking.

"I need to tell you what is happening at home. Some of Debbie's college friends are going to spend the summer traveling in the north eastern states and Canada. At first, her mother and I were hesitant about letting her go; but now, we think it might be a good idea. Perhaps this trip was in God's plans. The group will be gone over two months. You know time has a way of healing wounds.

The two men looked directly into each other's eyes as Mr. Peterson continued. "Since many in the church know about Debbie's disappointment and will be watching to see how things are between you and me, I want to suggest that we renew our friendship and stay as close as we ever were. As a matter of fact, Mildred has asked that you eat lunch with us next Sunday and she says you may bring Judith if you care to."

"Oh, no, no. I couldn't do that. I mean I want to eat with you, but I have decided that Judith will not come back to church for a while. Let's give this unfortunate episode time to subside."

He arose and started around the desk. Mr. Peterson stood and the two men faced each other. Scott extended his hand. "Sir, dear Sir, thank you so very much. I was praying the Lord would give us wisdom to handle this situation."

Mr. Peterson took Scott's hand and then, on impulse, drew the young pastor into his arms for a fatherly hug.

Aware of how big and strong, the six-foot-five Mr. Peterson was, Scott stepped back and grinned. "You know, Sir, I was a little afraid that you might want to punch me out, and I knew you could do it!"

Both men laughed as they headed toward the door.

Moments later, Scott leaned his back upon the closed door. Shutting his eyes, he whispered, "Thank you, Lord."

Then he moved over to the window to watch Mr. Peterson enter his car. He smiled as the older man lowered his head upon the steering wheel momentarily before starting the motor.

*C*hapter 11

The loud jangling of the alarm clock jarred Judith from a deep sleep, a sleep that had come only after hours of tossing and turning and thinking and thinking. She slipped out of bed and padded barefooted into the bathroom. Washing her hands, she looked down upon the ring on her left finger.

Suddenly, she did not want to go to school. On Saturday, she had been so very eager for Monday to come. She'd had grand visions of going into the teachers' lounge, displaying the ring to her friends, and hearing them gush over her engagement. Now, she could not feel the excitement. Her thoughts were troubled. Suppose things did not go right. Suppose Scott was pressured to change his plans. Suppose.... She splashed water upon her face and toyed with the idea of taking a "sick day." That idea, however, was dismissed almost immediately. Final exams were scheduled for the next week and she knew her students needed a thorough review of the semester's work. She had no choice; she had to go.

On purpose, she did not go to the lounge until almost time for the first bell. The room was filled with teachers discussing students or upcoming events.

"Well, there she is," Zack said. "We were worried about you.

You are usually our coffee maker, and we thought something must be wrong."

"Oh, I'm sorry about the coffee. I guess I'm running late," she said with a faint smile.

Seated on a nearby sofa, Mrs. Hendrix looked up and spied Judith's ring. She sprang up and shouted, "No wonder she's late! Look! Look! Judith is wearing an engagement ring! Our Judith is going to get married. Who's the lucky guy, Judith? Mike or Zack?" The question startled her.

As the teachers gathered around and raved, Judith glanced at Mike Moring. He stood, scowling at her with fierce anger in his eyes. He gritted his teeth and stormed from the room, making no attempt to hide his disgust.

Judith now looked at Zack. His eyes were sad but he tried to be pleasant. "Well, it's not I. That's all I can say. He's a lucky guy whoever he is. Best wishes, Judith," he said, turning away to gather his books. He did not wait to walk down the hall with her as he usually did.

Fighting back tears, Judith clutched her books to her chest and hurried down the hallway. *Lord, what have I done?* She thought of the reaction Scott's church had shown. *Is everyone against this wedding? Scott and I were so very sure that we had your leadership. What is wrong? Oh, dear Lord, I did not expect Mike and Zack to act this way.*

News of her engagement sped. Each period excited students hurried into the classroom, asking to see her ring and questioning her about her fiancé. Thankfully for Judith, the teenage enthusiasm carried her through the long day.

She ate lunch at her desk, not caring to see Mike or Zack. She had not anticipated their reactions to the announcement. She had considered both of them as dear friends, the best friends she had ever had; but now she wondered if they had viewed her in another light. She was remembering Mike's display of blatant anger and Zack's hurt look. In some way, she realized she had betrayed them. In all the time she had spent with them, she had never mentioned Scott. Perhaps, she had not mentioned him because her romance with Scott had moved so sporadically and so quickly. Now, with all her heart, she wanted to make things right with her two teacher friends; but, at this time, she knew she didn't have the strength to face another dilemma.

She was tormented by Mrs. Hendrix's strange question: "Who's the lucky guy, Judith? Mike or Zack?" How could she have been blind to what the other teachers were thinking? In what way had she given the impression that her relationship with the two single teachers had been more than friendship? She thought of Debbie Peterson and Scott's congregation who assumed that Debbie and Scott would marry. A strange saying flitted across her mind: "Love is blind, but the neighbors aren't." One thing, for sure, she had learned that the neighbors are always looking on! Looking on and making assumptions.

When the last bell rang, Judith gathered her books and slipped into the library. Pretending to check books in the far corner of the stacks, she waited until the halls were cleared and until the thirty-minute leaving time for teachers had passed. She did not want to encounter another person.

Scott had planned to drive to Cantrell Monday evening to discuss things with Judith. He wanted to assure her that everything would work out well. He could tell her about Mr. Peterson's visit and about Debbie's plans for the summer.

He was checking his schedule when the secretary buzzed his office and told him that Dr. Jeremiah Hudson was on the line. Happily, Scott picked up the phone. "Dr. Hudson!" he exclaimed. "How good to hear from you."

Dr. Hudson had been his favorite professor in seminary. Although Scott had not seen him for months, he had learned that Dr. Hudson had been promoted to Dean of Ministerial Students. Even before Dr. Hudson could respond, Scott added, "Congratulations, Dr. Hudson. I was glad to learn of your promotion. The ministerial students could not have a better person to lead them."

Dr. Hudson laughed. "Well, for sure, I'm talking to the exuberant Scott Jacobs! How are you, Son?"

"Fine," Scott said, "and how about you? By the way, where are you?"

"I'm in Zilford."

"Zilford?"

"Yes. I've come here for a conference and to see you personally. I will be tied up in meetings all during the day, but I really need to talk with you. Could you, please, meet me at the Holiday Inn at 6:30 for dinner? My plane will be leaving at ten o'clock."

There was no way Scott could say "No" to the elderly man who had meant so very much to him. He would have to rearrange his plans to see Judith.

"Of course, I'll meet you, Sir."

They talked for a few minutes before Dr. Hudson said, "I must go now. Have a good day, Scott. I'll see you at 6:30."

Scott rechecked his schedule, scratched out the word "evening" and scribbled in "Holiday Inn, 6:30." He would have to see Judith later.

Judith glanced at her watch. It was 3:30. Feeling that the building and the parking lot must be emptied, she headed for her car. As she neared her parking space, she was amazed to see Mike's red convertible next to her car. Mike stood, leaning against his car, arms folded over his chest. He straightened up as Judith approached.

"Hello, Mike," Judith said, trying to be casual.

"Hello," Mike said curtly. "Put your books in your car. I want to talk to you."

Something in his voice made Judith comply with no questioning. She turned to gaze up into Mike's face, noting a nervous twitch before he started speaking. "Judith Johnson, do you know what you did today?"

Judith shook her head.

"You humiliated me and you humiliated Zack. The three of us have spent time together almost every day for the last year or so; and yet, you walked in today with a ring on your finger. Neither Zack nor I knew that you were even dating anyone."

"That was because I had not really been dating."

"Not dating and yet you're getting married. Who are you kidding?"

"It is true. I have met Scott Jacobs off and on for several months. We have not dated, but we have known we were meant for each other from the day we met."

Seeing a hurt look upon Mike's face, Judith reached over and touched his arm. "I'm so sorry, Mike. I am sorry if I hurt you….. or Zack. I did not know that either of you cared for me in any special way. I thought we were just friends."

"Friends!" Mike almost snarled. "How could you have not known? Why do you think we spent so much time with you? Didn't you ever hear the things we said to you?"

"I always thought you were joking."

"Some joke. A joke on us. Didn't you know that we thought that you would, someday marry one of us?"

"No, I did not know. I'm so sorry. I really love both of you. You are the dearest friends I have ever had."

Mike turned and walked away. For a few minutes he paced back and forth in silence. He came back to face Judith.

"Can I change your mind?" he asked.

"No. I'm afraid not. I really want to marry Scott."

"Scott? Scott who? Tell me about him."

He stood looking into her eyes as she told him about the Zilford minister and their unusual love affair.

"Very well," he said at last. "I want you to be happy." He moved close to her. "Before I let you go, however, I want to kiss you goodbye." He did not wait for an answer but took her into his arms and kissed her. Because of her love and respect for him, Judith did not pull away. She let him kiss her. Then, looking up into his sad eyes, with instinct, she put her arms around him and hugged him.

She did not see the car parked across the street. She did not see Scott Jacobs as he started the engine and turned blindly to go back to Zilford.

Scott did not return to the church. He sped home. Having closed the blinds, he lay upon his bed, his eyes shut. For two hours, in grief he lay immobile, talking silently to the Lord.

He could not understand what was happening. Up until today, he had been so very sure of the Lord's leadership. Throughout his ministry, he had sought divine guidance during difficult situations and had seen definite answers to prayer. He thought he had learned to find the Lord's will. He had prayed about a wife and truly believed the Lord had picked out Judith Johnson. He remembered the morning he asked that the Lord would give him a wife with a keen sense of humor. In his mind again he saw Judith standing with a card in her hand, softly laughing aloud.

Turning his head to look at his bedside clock, abruptly he sat up. It was five o'clock. He was to meet Dr. Hudson at 6:30. Scott knew he must be there no later than 6:15, for the professor had taught him always to be at least fifteen minutes early for any appointment, a rule he had constantly followed.

Methodically as usual, he showered and dressed.

Chapter 12

Dr. Hudson was seated at a table in a secluded corner. He rose when he saw his former student enter the dining room. The two met mid-floor and shook hands warmly. Once again, Scott was impressed with Dr. Hudson's silver-streaked hair, winning smile, and gracious demeanor. Dr. Jeremiah Hudson, truly, was a prince among men.

"Scott Jacobs, how good to see you again," Dr. Hudson said.

"The honor is all mine, I assure you."

Dr. Hudson led Scott back to the table and indicated where he was to be seated. Scott noted the table was set for three but considered it an oversight. He sat across from Dr. Hudson.

"I've been eager to see you, Scott. For two years, I've followed your ministry very carefully. As a matter of fact, I drove by your church today. I see you've added another wing to your complex."

"Yes, Sir. We've added a gym. For the youth ministry, you know."

"And maybe for a school someday?"

"I 'm not sure about that, but the deacon board is giving the idea consideration."

They exchanged catch-up conversation until the waitress came to the table. "Are you ready to order now, Dr. Hudson?"

"I think so," he smiled as she placed the menus before them.

She returned to the table after several minutes and took their orders. The food came, and Scott became aware that he was hungry. In his eagerness to go to Cantrell, he had eaten only peanut butter crackers for lunch.

As they ate, they talked.

Dr. Hudson said, "Scott, I am here to talk with you about a new plan we are putting in at the seminary. We want you to be a part of that initial plan."

Scott's heart sank. He loved his church and hoped that Dr. Hudson was not going to offer him something that would take him away from Zilford.

Dr. Hudson detected the younger man's concern and said, "Don't worry. We're not going to take you away from your beloved church. We want to offer you something that will add to your ministry here."

Scott sighed. "Thank you, Sir. That is a relief. I was afraid you needed me to leave. I really feel I'm just getting started here."

Dr. Hudson continued. "Now that I am Dean of Ministerial Students, I'm instituting a new program. Each year before a student is graduated from the seminary, he must spend an internship with a selected pastor for a three-month summer period. Now, our committee has selected you to mentor one of our very best students. As a matter of fact, we have chosen you to mentor this student because this young man has made the whole faculty think of you."

Scott laughed. "I hope you mean that for good."

"Of course. Let me tell you something about this young man."

For the next half hour Dr. Hudson talked. The waitress came and cleared their places. Dr. Hudson looked up and said, "We'll wait for the dessert. We are expecting someone else at 8 o'clock." He looked at Scott and added. "We have this table reserved for the whole evening. It is Monday and we have been assured that our staying so long will not be a problem."

Scott glanced around. There were many empty tables. He relaxed, eager to hear about the young man who would be assigned to his church. Dr. Hudson began by saying that Caleb Barnett was an honor student who had only one semester left. He is devout. Teachable. Dependable. Exuberant. "Just like you," he said with a chuckle.

At twenty till eight, Dr. Hudson stood, smiling. Scott stood too, seeing a young man being directed to their table. He grinned. Dr. Hudson was right. The student could have been his brother. His hair and eyes were darker, but he was Scott's height, had a broad smile, and walked with Scott's eager stride. Before he reached the table he was extending his hand to Dr. Hudson and then to Scott. "I hope I haven't kept you fellows waiting," he said moving around the table to the empty place setting.

"Not at all," Dr. Hudson said. "You're early. Good boy. You are off to the right start. Scott here has never been late to anything in his life. Am I right?"

Scott acted as though he was questioning the comment, but then smiled.

Dressed in a purple housecoat and white bedroom shoes, Judith sat at the kitchen table, grading term papers. The stack seemed never ending. As she graded, periodically she glanced at the clock. She had expected Scott to call much earlier. She wanted to know what had happened during the day. Had people contacted him? Had they belittled his choice? Had they forgiven him for not choosing Debbie Peterson? Together, how were they going to proceed? She found it difficult to follow the reasoning of eleventh graders vainly trying to analyze Emerson's essays or Thoreau's stay in the woods. Personal questions tormented her mind.

Nine o'clock. Ten o'clock. Eleven o'clock. Judith could wait no longer. To face the teaching responsibilities of the next day, she knew she must get rest. Wearily, she placed the term papers in graded and ungraded stacks and checked her e-mail once again. Nothing from Scott. Disappointed, she turned off the lights, and stumbled through the dimly-lit hallway to her bedroom. She hoped for quick sleep.

Dear Lord, your Word teaches that you will keep me in perfect peace if my mind is stayed on Thee. I commit my love... my hurt... to you. I love you, Lord, and will thank you for seeing me through this time in my life.

It was after 11:00 that evening when Scott opened the door and led Caleb Barnett into the parsonage. After much discussion, it had been decided that Caleb would spend the week in Zilford to meet with the deacon board and to discuss the seminary's plan. Scott was confident that the deacons would approve. Already, they had discussed hiring an extra man to help with youth activities during the summer. It seemed to Scott that the Lord, himself, had picked the man for the job.

It was midnight when Scott sank into bed; and although he was exhausted, his mind jolted to thoughts of Judith in the arms of another man. He knew he would have trouble sleeping.

A week passed and Judith had not heard from Scott. She grieved that he had not called or even e-mailed her; yet she could not bring herself to make the first move. She still wore his ring but quickly changed the conversation when someone asked her about her plans.

"Oh, my," she said, "how can I think of anything right now other than getting through the end of school? I'm like Scarlet; I'll think of those things tomorrow."

It was her mother who gave her a nudge in the right direction. "Judith," she said. "Things are complicated for you and Scott at the moment; but given time, everything will work out all right, I'm sure. While you are waiting, why not do what you had planned to do earlier? Why not go back to the university and start working on your Master's degree? You have counted on doing that at some time. Maybe, this is the right time."

Judith did not answer, but her raised-eyebrows' expression led Mrs. Johnson to know she had given her daughter a possible solution.

Later in the evening, Judith opened her desk drawer, removed the university catalogue, and flipped to the pages earmarked graduate school.

Perhaps, her mother was right. For some reason, the timing seemed all wrong for her and Scott. Maybe, "time" is what they needed. Something was all wrong with their relationship, but what? She felt that she and Scott cared for each other, but how could she account for the days that she had not heard from him? No calls. No e-mails. No quick texts. Nothing.

She became thankful for the impending, last week of school, the harried days that teachers usually dreaded. Now, the thought of being inundated with exams to make and score, grades to average and record, and meetings to attend, gave her comfort. She would have little time to pine over personal matters.

With new determination, she searched through the college catalogue, making notes. Before turning off the lights and easing into bed, she had made a decision.. In two weeks, Scott or no Scott, she would be entering graduate school.

With matriculation papers in hand, Judith made her way to the Student Center to buy books for her courses. She was surprised to hear someone calling her name.

"Judith! Judith Johnson!"

She turned to see Mike Moring hurrying her way.

"What are you doing here?" he asked, glancing down at her left hand.

Noting his glance, Judith was thankful that she had not removed her ring. She had really considered leaving it at home, but now she was glad that she had not.

"I am here to start school. Why are you surprised? We discussed doing graduate work many times."

"Yes, but that was before you got engaged. I thought, maybe, that engagement had changed your plans. What does the Reverend think about your being away all summer?"

"I'm sure he has plenty to keep him busy. He will probably be glad to be rid of me for three months."

Mike walked beside her. "I'll go along and help you get your books. Believe me; you will need assistance carrying them to your dorm"

Judith sighed. "You know, I had forgotten how much walking a person has to do on campus."

"I'll say," Mike said, holding the door open.

With Mike's aid, Judith soon found books and supplies she needed. She insisted that she carry some of the load. To appease her, Mike took the heaviest books, leaving only the small bagged items.

As they trudged the long trip across campus to the Sigman Dorm, sweat tricked down Mike's forehead. With one free hand, Judith fumbled in her purse, trying to find a Kleenex. At the foot of the dorm's long stairway, she stopped. Looking up at Mike, she said. "Wait. Let me wipe the sweat from your face."

He smiled as she dabbed his brow and cheeks. "Now," she said, "come on up and I'll get you some iced tea or a cold Pepsi."

"Pepsi, if you please," Mike said, touching her elbow to lead her up the steps.

Once again, Scott Jacobs sat in a parking lot, watching a scene that wrenched his heart. Judy was there with the same man, wiping his face, and being led up the steps to her dorm.

What an idiot he was. Because of Granny Hansley's insistence, he had come to talk with Judith. Granny had been sure there was some explanation for what he had seen earlier.

"He could have been her brother or uncle or some family member," she had argued.

"No, Granny. He was a teacher I had seen before; and besides, he wasn't giving her a peck on the cheek. He was giving her an ardent kiss."

"Well, he might have been kissing her, but that does not mean she was kissing him back."

Scott had wanted to laugh at that remark but sadly said, "Granny, I saw her hug him after the kiss."

This discussion had taken place several times. Finally, Granny had persuaded him to find Judith and to talk with her.

Today, he had planned to do just that...to talk with Judith.... to hear her explain, but his plans were shattered. Again, he had found her with the same guy. Angrily, he turned the ignition key, but suddenly stopped. *"Father,"* he said as he searched for the dorm- room address Mrs. Johnson had scribbled. *"Father, I left once before without an explanation, but I'm not going to do that again. I'm going to knock on Judith's door and see her face to face. I'll confront her and whoever that guy is. If she is still wearing my ring, I'm going to tell her I love her and want her to be my wife. I'm going...."*

He had gone halfway up the cement steps when his cell phone sounded. He stopped and answered the call.

"Pastor," his secretary said in a sorrowful tone. "Granny Hansley has had a heart attack. She's in intensive care. I thought you would want to know."

He was running down the steps as he said, "I'll be right there."

Chapter 13

Pastor Jacobs stood a few feet from the bedside of his dearest, elderly friend. Granny Hansley lay still, her white hair brushed back from her pale face, her thin arms down by her side, monitoring machines clicking above. He watched as doctors and nurses ministered to her. Even when Granny answered questions asked by the doctor, she kept her eyes closed and whispered labored responses. At times, he saw a doctor shake his head or a nurse give a discouraging glance. Yet, Scott stood and prayed silently.

The doctor went to the door. "Reverend Jacobs," he said, "may I speak with you?"

Outside the room, the doctor said, "I understand the Mrs. Hansley has no living relatives. Is that true?"

"Yes, as far as I know," Scott answered, "but she has a host of church friends. As a matter of fact, they have been having constant prayer sessions for her."

"Well, that may account for what has happened. When Mrs. Hansley came in two hours ago, her heart attack had been so massive that we gave her very little chance of surviving. Thankfully, she is now responding rather well. I tell you, Reverend; I am confident prayer does change things. In my twenty years as a doctor, over and over I have seen prayers answered. I've seen things happen when there could be no earthly explanation. Someday when we have time, let's sit down over a cup of coffee, and I'll tell you some miraculous cases."

The doctor had started walking down the hall; so Scott moved along with him. "Sir, I would count it a privilege to hear your stories. Call me whenever you have a free hour anytime, night or day."

"I may take you up on that sometime at midnight when I'm having to stay awake."

"Good. My number is in the book."

The doctor stopped a few feet from the nurses' center. "We have more tests and X-rays to make before we know what procedure we should follow. Because of Mrs. Hansley's age, the decision will be a difficult one. Please check to see if she has any relatives. We may need their consent."

Later in the day, Scott entered Granny's room. She was awake. Scott was happy to see a slight pinkness in her cheeks

Taking the hand that did not have an IV, he said, "Granny, you know you gave all of us a scare."

"I'm sorry, Pastor," she said slowly, each word with effort. "You know I didn't plan this. I have too much to do to be lying in bed." She paused, stopped talking, and breathed heavily with her eyes closed.

"You just lie there and take it easy, Granny. You'll be good as new soon."

Granny opened her eyes. "I 'm glad......you are here, Pastor. I want you...... to do something for me," she whispered.

"You name it."

"I want you to....... call Judith Johnson. Tell her. ......I want to see her. Will you do that?"

He started to protest; but seeing the troubled expression in Granny's faded blue eyes, he changed his mind. "Of course, Granny. I'll call her as soon as I get back to the church." He knew he would have to get the dorm's phone number.

Judith answered the phone and swayed when she heard Scott's voice. She sank upon a chair and said, "Hello, Scott. How are you?"

"I'm fine, Judith, but I'm afraid I'm a bearer of bad news." He hesitated. He thought he heard her catch her breath. "Granny Hansley has had a heart attack."

"Ohhhh, I am so very sorry," Judith whispered, remembering the sweet, little lady who had promoted her love for Scott.

"She wants to see you, Judith. That's why I called you. Granny is in intensive care; and, to be honest, she can't have visitors. So far, I'm the only person who has been allowed to see her. But if it is important for her to talk with you, I'll see if the doctor will give you permission."

Without hesitation, Judith said, "I'll be there this evening. And, Scott, thank you for calling." She held the phone close to her heart even after Scott hung up.

When Judith entered the intensive care's waiting room, she was awed to see so many people she had seen at Community Church. She wanted to shrink from the room, especially when all eyes were turned her way. Her despair was abated only because Mr. Peterson spied her and hurried across the room.

"Hello, Judith," he said warmly as though she were a close friend. "We're sorry to be seeing you again under such sad circumstances. As you can see," he said as he motioned toward the church members, "we all love Granny Hansley."

Noting her shy glance over the crowd, Mr. Peterson added, "Pastor Jacobs is with her now. He's the only person being admitted into intensive care." He checked his watch. "Visitation hour is almost over. Pastor should be out soon."

"Thank you," Judith said quietly and took a seat in a nearby chair.

She was relieved when Scott appeared, stopping just outside the door. Church members moved close to hear his report, but Judith sat still, her heart beating strangely. Once again, she was aware how much she loved Scott Jacobs. As she watched, she wished she were standing by his side.

When he had finished talking, Scott glanced across the room. He saw Judith. In a moment, his inner composure was shattered. *Judith Johnson. I should be angry with you. I should hate.... no, no a Christian can't hate. I just don't understand you.* A frown furrowed his brow; and yet, his attitude changed immediately when he noted the sweet gleam in Judith's eyes. A few quick steps and he was standing before her, pulling her up, and holding her two hands to his chest. Judith's eyes filled with tears. She could not speak. In her heart, she knew that, no matter what had happened, that she and Scott loved each other. Scott squeezed her hands. "Judith, I didn't know you were here. Thank you so much for coming."

"I wanted to be here," she said. "How is Granny?"

"She's hanging in there. The doctor says she's a real fighter. It's too early, however, to know the damage done to the heart."

"I'm so very sorry," Judith said.

"I know," Scott said. "You have not known her for very long; but already she is in your heart. Look around, Judith. These people genuinely love Granny, for she has been in the church for as long as they can remember. She was a charter member, you know. Yes, Granny has babied most of these people the way she has babied us." He said the last sentence softly, searching Judith's face to see if she understood what he was saying.

Judith did not speak but looked into Scott's eyes and nodded.

Scott smiled. He wanted to take Judith into his arms, to hold her close.

How long, how long, heavenly Father, before Judith can be my wife? I love her. I need her. I want her now. Please. He was remembering that earlier that day he had talked with the Lord, claiming Psalm 37:4 : **"Delight thyself also in the Lord; and he shall give thee the desires of thine heart."** *Lord, you know I delight in you every day of my life and you know the desire of my heart. I want to marry Judith Johnson. I have been so very sure that you picked her to be my wife. Why are things not working out?*

Mindful of watchful eyes upon them, Scott gently touched Judith's elbow and said, "Come with me. She eased beside him, and for an hour, they moved from one group to another. With each group, Scott led in prayer. No one could have guessed that Scott and Judith were having troubles.

At length, Scott looked at his watch and said. "Judith, it is getting late. I know you need to go. It will take at least thirty minutes for you to get back home. I don't like for you to be on the highway late at night." Judith loved the last comment. *He is protective. He wants to take care of me, just as Dad did my mom. He hasn't been calling me, but he loves me, I know.*

"I'll walk you to your car," he said.

"Oh, Pastor," a soft voice said. "If you are walking with Miss Johnson to the parking lot, may I, please, walk with you? I had to park in the farthest lane. I suppose you have heard about some of the recent trouble in the parking area. I'm really afraid to go alone. I have been waiting for someone to leave so that I could tag along."

Scott turned. "Why, of course, Mrs. Howard, we would be glad to have you walk with us."

Judith smiled and nodded. *Accompanying Mrs. Howard is the right thing to do, of course, but I did want to be alone with Scott for a few precious minutes.*

In the hallway, Scott walked between the two ladies, consciously, touching Judith's side as they walked. Even this slight touch made his heart beat faster. When he was in Judith's presence, it was as though an electrical current drew them together. He wanted to put his arm around her shoulder, to tilt his head to smell the fragrance of her shampoo, to take her into his arms and to kiss her.

He wanted to do show his love, but things were not working out as he had hoped. He was further disappointed, for they reached Judith's car first, and the two of them had to say goodbye, even without a gentle hug.

Chapter 14

Scott called the next day to explain that Granny, with belabored breathing, had whispered another request to see Judith. "I don't know why she is so insistent that you come, Judith; but if you can, I'm sure she will appreciate it."

"Of course, I can come," Judith said. "My classes have not started yet; I can be there all afternoon. In fact, if I can find a place to stay, I'll remain overnight so that I can be with her until bedtime and then all day tomorrow."

Scott was pleased. *You are going to make a wonderful preacher's wife; that is, if you actually end up being my wife.* He was constantly tormented by the pictures of Judith kissing another man...of Judith entering her dorm with the same man.

When Judith arrived that afternoon, she found Scott in a corner lounge chair, reading a book. She smiled as he glanced up, noisily closed the book, and headed her way. They met near the floor-to-ceiling windows where he took her two hands and held them to his chest. That was a gesture he had done before and she loved it. Looking up into his hazel blue eyes, she tried to read the kind of message he had to give.

"How is she? Is she any better?" she asked.

Scott shook his head. "Not yet, but she's hanging in there.

Her doctor says she's a real fighter. You know what it means, however, when they say, 'We are doing all we can.'"

It was almost five o'clock when the doctor checked in on Granny and gave permission for Judith to have a brief visit. Remembering Scott's description of Granny's gaunt appearance, Judith crept into the room, dreading to look upon her friend.

"Hello, dear," she whispered as she touched Granny's limp, white hand. *Oh, my, I never noticed those huge blue veins. You look so little and frail. I am so very sorry.*

Granny opened her eyes with a slight, happy flickering as she saw Judith. She opened her mouth but made no sound.

"Don't feel you have to talk, Granny. I just wanted you to know that I'm here; and if I find a place to stay, I'll be with you all weekend."

Granny shook her head. "I want you...... to stay at my house. Key next door. Scott can..... take you. Understand?"

"Yes, Granny, I understand. That would be wonderful. I would count it a privilege to stay in your home. I'll do as you have asked. I'll get Scott to take me there. Thank you so very much. I did want to stay in Zilford until you could go home."

A restful smile settled on Granny's face as she closed her eyes and slightly nodded her head. Judith sat quietly by her bed.

When Scott arrived, she told him Granny's wish. "Isn't that sweet?" she said.

"Yes, it is just what Granny would do."

"She wants to talk with me tomorrow."

"What about?"

"She did not say."

Scott helped Judith with her coat and led her into the hallway.

"I think you need to follow me to Granny's house," he said. "I'll be gone all day tomorrow and you will need your car."

Judith knew that Scott was right, but she wished she could ride with him. Perhaps they could talk and dispel whatever had come between them in the last few weeks.

Thankfully, traffic was light, giving Judith freedom to note turns and landmarks. She needed to know how to get back to the hospital.

In ten minutes, Scott slowed down at a street light and pointed to a stately, white two-storied home with four massive columns and a wrap-around-porch. Low-cut shrubbery, blooming flowers, and a decorative white fence seemingly tucked the house away from the street. Judith noted two children's swings hanging from a massive tree in the side yard. *I thought the Hansleys had no children. Wonder why they would have swings.*

Scott waited for Judith to pull into the driveway ahead of him, then hurried from his car to open her door. As she stepped out, she lingered by the car, being enthralled by the closeness to this man she loved, wanting to stay there with him forever. Scott, too, seemed reluctant to move. His true impulse was to take Judith into his arms, in spite of the hurt she had caused him. Instead, he turned and opened the car's back door and took out Judith's overnight bag.

He led her to the front porch. "Stay here, Judith. I have to go next door to get the key." He cut across the yard and through an opening in the hedges, an opening Granny and her neighbor had enjoyed for years.

When he returned and unlocked the door, he said, "May I go in and show you around? I've been to this house many times, you know." With a sheepish grin, he added, "I even know where Granny keeps the coffee just in case you would like to make a pot for us."

"I'm not a very good coffee maker, but I'll try," Judith said, happy that he was going inside.

While the coffee perked, Scott walked her through the house, commenting about each room, and opening closet doors as though he were checking things before leaving her alone.

"She usually has some good, homemade cookies in this jar," Scott said as Judith poured the coffee. He set the yellow cookie jar on the table and reached into a cabinet for two small dishes. "Now, you sit there and I'll sit here. We'll leave Granny's place just as though she is here. She would like that."

They sat across from each other, suddenly very quiet. Tears welled up in Judith's eyes. Finally she said, "Oh, Scott, what has happened? What has come between us?"

He frowned. "You don't know?"

"No, I don't know. You have not called me or contacted me in any way since that day in your church. Did your church people disapprove of me so greatly? Did they turn you against me?"

"My church people have nothing to do with what has come between us."

"Then what? I thought we loved each other."

"I thought so, too, until you changed everything."

"What do you mean? What have I done?"

"I might as well tell you. Granny will as soon as she is strong enough. I am sure that's what she wants to talk with you about."

"What? What have I done?"

Her innocence angered him. "As if you do not know!"

"I do not know. Please explain to me."

"Okay, Judith, I'll explain. The day after we announced our engagement and the Petersons acted the way they did, Mr. Peterson came to see me and we got things straightened out. I went to Cantrell that afternoon to tell you about Mr. Petterson's visit and to tell you about my new assistant."

"You were in Cantrell? I didn't see you."

"No, you did not see me, but I saw you! I saw you in the parking lot kissing that Mike Moring guy!"

"Ohhhh." Judith sank back in her chair. "Oh, Scott, that kiss meant nothing to me."

"Really? That is what Granny said. She insisted there was an explanation. She nagged me day by day until I decided to see you. To my surprise, I learned you were going to summer school; so I rode over to the university. I wanted to tell you that Debbie came by to say goodbye; and when she met my assistant, she completely forgot I existed. I thought everything was finally all right. But I was wrong!" His eyes narrowed. "Do you know why, Judith? I went to the university, and there I saw the same Mike Moring carrying your books and going into your dorm with you. That was it! I knew then your love for me had been a farce."

Judith reached across the table and touched Scott's hands. "Oh, Scott. You are wrong. I love you. I love you with all my heart."

"Then explain Mike Moring to me."

"That day at school, Mike was waiting for me in the parking lot. He was upset because so suddenly I was wearing your ring. I told him how I met you and that I loved you. At first he was angry and then he said that he understood and asked if he could kiss me goodbye. I did not give my consent, but he just pulled me to him and kissed me."

"Come on, Judith. I saw you hug him after the kiss."

"You are right. I did hug him. I hugged him because I had caused him hurt. I had not meant to. I did not know he thought of me as more than a friend. I hugged him because I was sorry for what I had done."

"Well, how about your sudden decision to go back to school and to the same school, evidently, Mike is attending? And what was he doing going up into your dorm?"

"Until that day, I did not know that Mike was there. We had talked about going back to get out Master's degrees, but I did not know he was going this year. It just happened. He saw me on campus and helped me carry my books and supplies. I was still wearing your ring. He…"

"Judith, don't be naive. That ring meant nothing to him."

"Yes, it did, Scott. When you know Mike better, you'll know that's true." She sat up straight and stared across the table. "Mike is not the issue, Scott. Either you and I love each other, or we don't. Do you love me?"

"Of course, I love you. That is why this whole Mike Moring thing has driven me insane."

Judith reached across the table and touched Scott's hands. "Oh, Scott, I love you. I am sorry if I have caused you any worry. I will always love you and only you."

They were up and around the table. They held each other close. With her head resting against his chest, Scott breathed the fragrance of Judith's shampoo – a fragrance he had cherished since the first day he met her.

Glancing at the kitchen clock, Scott tilted Judith's face. "I hate to leave you, Judith, but it's late and I must be on the road at dawn tomorrow. I'll be traveling to Charlotte for a conference. Anyhow, you need a good night's sleep." He cupped her face in his hands and brushed his lips across her lips. "How about walking me to the door?"

At the door, he kissed her long and tenderly. She slipped her arms up around his neck and responded. He left with a lightness he had not felt since the day he first asked Judith to be his wife.

Chapter 15

Judith argued with herself about going to summer school. Now that Granny was in critical condition, she did not want to leave Zilford. She wanted to be with Scott and his concerned people. *I am angry with myself. I did not want to start graduate work yet. I enrolled, simply, because things were going so poorly with Scott and me. I do not know how I made such a foolish decision. Oh, yes, now I know. Mother suggested it. I suppose she was trying to help. She saw how miserable I was.*

She talked with Scott. "Honey, I am thinking about cancelling my plans to start graduate studies this session. I probably will get a Master's degree someday, but I'm in no hurry. You see," she said, "when we are married and have Jude and...."

"Joseph," he said.

"Yes, Joseph, and John and Megan and Susan and many more, I do not want to work. I want to be a stay-at-home mom."

"That's fine, Judith. I would like to have you near me during that time in our lives. You have considered, however, that you will probably lose the money you have paid the university."

"I've thought about that, but it doesn't matter. I'll count the money a gift to my alma mater."

"You could do that, or, maybe, you could allow someone to go in your place. Why don't you check with the Dean to see if there is some needy student who would love the opportunity to go to summer school?"

Judith's eyes brightened. "Oh, that is a great idea. I didn't think of that. I'll call and make an appointment with Dean Darnell today.

Since Granny remained in intensive care for nine days, Judith spent practically all of her time in the waiting lounge, quietly speaking with tearful people who came by, just to get a report, knowing ahead of time that they could not see the patient.

Judith, herself, had been able to go into Granny's room only twice a day. Each time her heart sank when she looked down at Granny's ashen face and thin arms. Fighting tears, she held Granny's hand, talking very little and encouraging Granny not to talk. After each short visitation, she went back into the waiting room and spent time with the numerous church members who always seemed to be there. Strangely, a bond seemed to exist between her and these Community Church people, almost as though they now accepted her as an extension of the pastor. *Granny would love this,"* she thought. *"I'll tell her someday."*

Once, when the waiting room was almost empty, Judith noted a middle aged woman who sat quietly between two teenaged girls. A teenaged boy paced around the room and stopped now and then to talk with the lady. Judith assumed the four made up a family. She walked over and introduced herself. "My name is Judith Johnson." She hesitated, wondering if she should add, "I'm the pastor's fiancée." She did.

The young man grinned. "We know that. We were in church the Sunday Pastor Jacobs made the announcement."

"We are the Barber Family," the woman said, extending her hand.

Judith shook Mrs. Barber's hand and said, "Do you mind if I sit with you a while? It seems most of our friends have gone home."

Already, the young man was pulling up a chair facing his mother and sisters. He found another chair and placed it near Judith. Smiling, Judith asked, "Did you have a close relationship with Granny?"

"Oh, yes, we surely did," Mrs. Barber said. "As a matter of fact, she came to be called Granny because of these three children?

"Really? How was that?" Judith possessed a knack for drawing people into conversations. She asked this question and eased back into her chair, silently inviting an answer.

One of the girls said, "We lived with Granny for several months one time. Bobby was four, Hannah was three, and I was a baby. As a matter of face, as Mama said, we were the ones who started calling Mrs. Hansley "Granny," and Mama says the name stuck.

"Yeh," Bobby said. "Pretty soon the whole church called her Granny. Even the pastor called her Granny!"

The mother explained, "Mrs. Hansley didn't mind that name at all. Her hair was barely turning gray then; and even though she was youthful, she liked being called Granny. You see, she and Mr. Hansley never had any children."

Mrs. Barber looked inside her pocket book and took out a twenty dollar bill and handed it to Bobby. "Would you kids like to go to the cafeteria to get something to eat? We might be here another hour or so."

"You bet!" Bobby said, moving his chair back and motioning for his sisters to follow him.

When they were gone, Mrs. Barber said, "I would like to tell you how we happened to live with the Hansleys for such a long time, but I would rather talk about it without the children. They were so very young then that they do not remember exactly why we were there."

Understanding, Judith nodded her head. Her eyes pleaded for the rest of the story.

Mrs. Barber continued, "My husband and I were young and we had these three wonderful children. We were very happy until Bart started hanging around with some men at the plant where he worked. He started drinking with them, at first only a beer and later more and more. Eventually, he began coming home drunk. Now, you might not know, but some men drink and become silly; but some become angry and mean. Sadly, Bart was one of those whose personality changed for the worse. He ranted and raged, threatening the children and me."

"I'm sorry," Judith said

"Please don't' get me wrong. When Bart was sober, he was the sweetest, kindest man you could know. It was just that alcohol did something awful to him. One evening..." She stopped in mid-sentence. "I don't know why I am telling you this."

Judith reached over and touched Mrs. Barber's hand. "Sometimes it helps to share things."

With tears filling her eyes, Mrs. Barber started again, "One evening, when Bart became abusive, I feared for our children. He was throwing things, something that he had never done before, causing our terrified children to hide behind the couch, sobbing. I took my baby, snatched the car keys, and ran to the car, calling the little ones to follow. I wanted them to be safe. We had no family near us and I had little money. Aimlessly, I drove thirty miles and came into Zilford with nowhere to go. I spied the church and drove into the parking lot. I thought we would be safe there during the night.

"We were sitting quietly in the car when suddenly there was a tap on my window. I was scared almost to death; but when I turned and looked, there was a man at my door. He stepped backward a couple feet and smiled.

"I rolled my window down a couple inches and waited for him to speak. I knew he could hear the children crying."

"Young lady," he said. "My name is Philip Hansley. I'm a deacon in this church. Is there any way we can help you?"

"I do not know why I did it, but I opened my door, got out, and began crying. Well, that night Philip Hansley took my children and me into his home. His wife prepared a meal for us and later settled us in a large bedroom upstairs.

"I would give you two rooms," Mrs. Hansley explained, "but I thought all of you might like to sleep in the same room tonight."

"And that's how you came to know the Hansleys?" Judith said.

"Yes, but, Miss Johnson, that is not the best part. Mr. Hansley went to see my husband every day for a week." Her eyes brightened as she went on to explain how he helped to sober her husband and to encourage him to get help at a Christian rehab home where he stayed three months. It was during that time that her husband came to a saving knowledge of Christ. Mrs. Barber stood to say, "And would you believe, in our church now my husband. is a wonderful Bible teacher."

With a natural impulse, Judith stood to give Mrs. Barber a hug.

Scott had come into the waiting room as Judith talked with Mrs. Barber. He smiled. *Isn't she great? People gravitate to her. They tell her things they had not told anyone. Watching her now, I know why. She is a good listener. Yes, she really knows how to listen.*

At that moment, someone tapped him on the shoulder. "Reverend Jacobs, you are wanted in the emergency room." Scott turned immediately and sped from the room unnoticed.

In the long, empty hallway, the intern led the way, his rubber-soled shoes lightly squeaking in time with the clicking noise of Scott's leather-soled loafers.

Turning his head to Scott as they ran along, the intern explained that a young man had shot his young friend while hunting.

"Do you know the boys' names?" Scott asked.

"One is a Jones boy and the other, a Markham, I think.

"Which one was shot?"

"The Jones boy. I know because the doctor called a Mrs. Gilbert Jones to tell her about her son."

"That's sad. Mrs. Jones just lost her husband five months ago, and that boy is her only child. How bad is it? Do you know?"

Both men were slightly winded now as they turned down the last hall to the emergency room. "I don't' really know how bad it is. The kid had splatters of blood on his chest and right arm. Pellets spread like that, but sometimes they don't do too much damage.

Thankfully, he didn't get hit in the face."

A touch to a huge, wall button and the emergency doors flung open. Scott stood at the operation door, staring through the little window. Dr. Green, a member of the Community Church hovered over Billy Jones with another doctor and nurse. He glanced up, said something to the other doctor and walked toward Scott.

"Pastor, it's the Jones boy. So far, it doesn't look as though he is in much danger. The pellets are not buried deep, and we think we can pick them out. I called you down because Mrs. Jones is on her way, and I thought she might need you when she gets here. She is still grieving over her husband, you know."

"Is Billy awake?"

"We have sedated him, but he will probably recognize you if

you want to go over and speak to him. Just stay out of the way. Okay?" Scott nodded and mouthed, "Thank you."

When Scott returned to the waiting area outside the emergency room, he saw sixteen-year-old Pete Markham, sitting with his elbows burrowed into his knees, his face in his hands.

He walked over to the boy and sat down beside him. Pete glanced up, and seeing the pastor, began to cry. Scott put his arm around Pete, pulled him over, and allowed him to cry on his shoulder.

The door opened and a pale, wide-eyed mother rushed into the room. Scott eased away from Billy and hurried to her. "He's all right, Mildred. He's all right. I've seen him and have had prayer with him. He had a little hunting accident; and, Mildred, he caught a few pellets, but the doctor is removing them now. He'll be fine." He patted her back.

"Oh, thank the Lord, Pastor!"

She turned and looked at the youngster who sat bent over his knees, sniffling. "Pastor, is that Pete Markham? Is he the one who shot Billy?"

"Yes," the pastor said, "but he didn't mean to do it. Both boys knew that it is not hunting season; but yesterday Pete received a rife for his birthday, and the two guys went out only for target practicing.

"Pete said that Billy suggested they separate just to see how far apart they would be when they were hunting together. They were about 25 feet from each other when they spooked a covey of birds. As the birds shot up noisily, Pete, in his excitement, slung his gun around and fired. When Billy cried out, Pete realized what he had done. He screamed and threw down his gun. Frantic, he pulled out his cell phone and dialed 911. He was crying so hard that the operator had difficulty getting the information; however, the rescue squad was there within ten minutes. Your Billy really did get immediate care."

Mrs. Markham took a tissue from her purse and wiped her eyes. "I suppose I should go talk with Pete," she said. "I know he is hurting, too. I'm sure he did not mean to hurt Billy. These boys are very close friends. They are like brothers."

When Scott returned to the intensive care unit, he found Judith alone. He was glad, for he wanted to tell her about Billy and Pete. She listened wide-eyed, making little "oh-my" murmurings from time to time. At length, he looked at her thoughtfully and said, "Judith, if you marry me, and I hope you will, you do know what kind of life we'll live together, don't you? We will be sharing heartaches and burdens of a big church family every day. Can you do that?"

"Yes, I think I can with the Lord's help, of course."

Scott smiled at her. *Father, she is going to make a perfect pastor's wife.* He started to tell her so, but she moved close to him; and with a twinkle in her eyes, said, "By the way, Scott, we will also be sharing joyful weddings, births, graduations, anniversaries, and hundreds of birthdays. I will love that. I like ice cream and cake."

Chapter 16

J udith was disappointed that she saw Scott so very seldom. Usually, he came to the hospital once daily. Sometimes, however, his schedule was so filled that he sent his assistant pastor or Youth Leader Caleb in his place.

As a rule, all six members of the Community Church staff reported to work each morning at 8:30. After a brief meeting and prayer in the pastor's office, they scattered to their individual offices for private devotions and daily planning. By 9:30, the church was abuzz with activity that did not stop until quiting time - 3:00 for the ministers and 4:00 for the secretaries. The Senior Pastor took into consideration that the associate ministers did much of their work in the evenings, meeting with various groups and visiting in homes.

Judith knew all of this, but her heart still longed for Scott. Seeing him for a few brief minutes in the waiting room did not suffice. There, with so many people around, the two could only steal glances at each other, hoping their eyes would speak what was in their hearts.

Granny came off the critical list the tenth day. "If she does well tonight," Dr. Higgins said, "she will be moved into a private room tomorrow."

"That is wonderful," Judith said. "Will she be able to have visitors?"

"Only a few. Let's not push things yet," the doctor said. "I'll let you and Reverend Jacobs choose a few to visit each day. You, two, talk it over and pick out her closest friends – maybe someone who has lived in Hansley Haven.

Hansley Haven?

Dr. Higgins made a step-back gesture. "You mean you do not know about the Hansley Haven?"

"I guess not. I saw a sign near the porch, but I thought the wording was just a personal choice. I did not know there was any significance to the name, Hansley Haven.

Dr. Higgins lowered his head slightly, looking over the tops of his small glasses. With a slow smile, he said, "Oh, yes, there is a significance. The name really grew out of the many, hurting people who have lived in that house. Someone along the way dubbed it "Hansley Haven."

"Come with me," the doctor said, winking and heading to the door. "I want to show you something." The wink was unusual for Dr. Higgins. Although he was a surgeon with many accolades, he never seemed to be happy. He was married and had grown children, but his demeanor was always solemn, even sad. Judith had noticed his troubled expression right away the first time he came into Granny's room. *Wake up, Granny,* she wanted to say. *This doctor has a need. Maybe, you can help him.* Even then, she whispered a silent prayer for Dr. Thurman Higgins.

She followed the physician into the waiting room, thinking, *"How can he possibly show me anything about Hansley Haven?"*

The doctor spanned the room of about fifteen people sitting quietly or standing in groups, talking. He cleared his throat. "May I have your attention, please."

When all eyes were turned upon him, he forced a smile and

said, "How many of you people are here to learn about Mrs. Hansley?" At least ten people raised their hands. "I see," he said, "and how many of you ten or so have lived in Hansley Haven?" The same hands were raised again.

Judith's jaw dropped for a second. Dr. Higgins glanced her way and cocked his head slightly. "See," he said quietly. He turned and spoke again. "We are happy to report if all goes well, Mrs. Hansley will be going to a private room tomorrow and we will be allowing short visits, especially to you who have lived in her home." He slightly bowed and left the room, aware of a thank-you chorus.

Scott called Judith on her cell phone. "Judith, I'm free tonight. Let's go to the Olive Garden for dinner. I surely would like to be alone with you for a while. I miss you. Just knowing you are right here in Zilford and I see you so very seldom drives me crazy!"

"I miss you, too, Honey; and I have so much to tell you. I think I'm going to write a book, yes a book about Hansley Haven, and I want your help. I've always known I wanted to write a book, and now I believe I have the right subject."

Two days later Judith entered the waiting area and spied a tall, stalwart young man whom she had seen raise his hand at Dr. Higgins' request. She debated going to speak with him. *Father, lead me. Is this an entry for my book? What story does this young man have to tell?* She felt a nudge, an inner urge. Picking up her newly-bought notebook and a pen, she crossed the room to where the young man sat. When he saw her approaching, he stood immediately. His quick rising and stance made Judith think that he might salute her. *This young man definitely has military training.* He made her think of her Marine uncle.

Judith extended her hand and said, "Hi. My name is Judith

Johnson. I am a Granny Hansley's friend.. I saw you here the other evening when Dr. Higgins asked for the hand show. I am thinking about writing a book about Hansley Haven and I wondered if you would care to tell me about your stay there."

The young man gave her a broad smile, producing two deep dimples in his cheeks. "My name is Stan Steelman and I would be delighted to tell you about my time with the Hansleys. Mr. and Mrs. Hansley saved my life.

"Ooooh," was all that Judith said.

Stan continued, "You see, I was one of the first Marines sent to Iraq. Judith, pardon me for saying this, but it is true: War is Hell. His chin quivered. I saw things there that I cannot tell you about. Not now, at least.

"My best buddy was killed by a roadside bomb. When I rushed to the scene, I saw his arm, his leg, his…." Stan's voice trailed off and he lowered his head, trying to hide the tears that threatened to spill from his eyes. "After Ben died, I endured five months of hourly horror. Every day I expected to be wounded or to die. Eventually my being-wounded nightmare became a reality. While I was on a routine mission, a fiery roadside blast killed two of my men and sent me to the hospital in critical condition. No matter what they did for me, my body would not stop shaking. My head constantly felt as though it would explode. Finally, the doctors deemed it wise to send me back to the states. They gave me an honorable discharge. Shell shock, they called it.

"I'm so very sorry," Judith said as she slipped her hand over to cover his clenched fist.

"Thank you," he whispered. "Well, I came back to the states, but I was a mess. I went home to my parents and my two younger brothers, but I could not function normally. Any loud noise sent me screaming and scrambling for cover. Once, my little brother was playing a simple war game. When I heard shots, I ran through the house, knocking my family members down, crying for them to take cover. This is the kind of thing I did over and over. It was so bad that my family began walking around, watching me with fear in their eyes.

"One day, my dad took me out on the porch and talked with me.

"Son," he said, "your mom and I love you with all our hearts and we really want to help you; however having you here at home is not working. Your mom and the boys are terrified when you lose control. Now, I know you cannot help those outbursts. War has devastated your body and mind. I am grieved about that. Please understand. We have tried to rehabilitate you; but, Son, we do not know how. I really think it would be best for the family, and for you, if you were to go to a Veteran's Hospital where you can get professional help.

"For the first time in my life, I saw my father crying. I knew then I had to do something. I agreed that he was right and promised to go to the VA for help. Two days later, I packed my things and left, assuring them I was checking in a nearby VA hospital. I hugged and cried with each of my family members, thinking I would not see them again on earth. I really planned to kill myself. The unending misery was more than I could bear.

I wanted to use a gun, but my dad had removed all pistols and hunting rifles from our home. I knew he had done that because of me.

"I went to a nearby park and sat on a picnic table. I wanted to end my life, but I wanted to be found, hopefully, to give my folks some closure. From my duffle bag, I took out a pad and wrote personal letters to my parents and my two brothers. I put their names on their separate envelopes and sealed them. It was time for me to end it all. I was scrambling through my shaving equipment to find a razor blade when, out of nowhere, it seemed, a man walked up and touched my shoulder.

"I turned and that was the first time I saw Mr. Hansley. 'May I?" he said as he eased up onto the table, without waiting for an answer, and began talking with me. I'll give you more details about that conversation someday if you want me to. Right now, I want to tell you what happened.

"Mr. Hansley talked me into going home with him. He and his wife – Granny as we now call her - fed me a wonderful meal and encouraged me to tell them what had been happening in my life. They hovered over me like doting grandparents, giving me tender love. I didn't know why, but I completely opened up to them. I told them everything. When it was bedtime, they did a strange thing; they took my hands and prayed. I had never held hands and prayed before. I liked it." Judith smiled. Holding hands had been new for her, too. "That night I slept alone upstairs where, I guess you know, there are four huge bedrooms." Judith smiled and nodded. Stan pressed his lips tightly together twice before he spoke again. "Unfortunately, that night I kept having flashbacks that made me leap from my bed and pace the floor. I'm sure they must have heard me."

Stan stopped and asked Judith, "Did you notice there is a bedroom across from the master bedroom? She nodded. "Well, that room used to be Brother Hansley's study. But, do you know what he did? He wanted me to be close to him; so, the next day, he had some guys from the church come over to move his desk and files to another room. He put a bed in the study and had me sleep there close to his room. He wanted me to be near him. Many nights he spent hours sitting by my bed, calming me down"

For the first time, Judith interrupted, "Did you ever get professional help?"

"Absolutely! Brother Hansley took me to the Butler facilities and stayed with me through every step of the way. I remained at the Hansley's home, but I went to daily sessions at the VA. It took a long time and a lot of prayers to bring me back to normal, but the Hansleys and their Haven saved my life. By the way, Judith, I was the one who named the house Hansley Haven and had the sign made. I did it almost as a joke, but the Hansleys loved it and would not let me take it down."

Judith wiped the tears from her eyes. "Thank you for sharing your story with me," she said, "and thank you for serving our country in the Iraqi cause. You may not know the good you have done; but even today, many Iraqis are rising up to praise you for their freedom. The Lord bless you, Stan." She knew she would write his story and was sure she would, first, present it to Stan for approval.

Scott called late in the afternoon. He sounded excited. "Judith, I have had a brain storm. You know, how careful we have had to be about my spending time with you alone in the Hansley Haven. Well, I have a solution. I have talked with my two secretaries today and they can come over and spend a couple nights. They really do have to get everything in order, you know. Granny is getting to go home this weekend. What do you think? Would you like some company?"

"Like some company? Yes, especially YOU! Do you think we could go and sit in the parlor, like on a real date?"

Scott laughed. "Yes, and I'll dare my secretaries to disturb us." He became serious. "Judith, do you realize we have had the most unorthodox courtship in history? Here, we are ready to get married, and I have held you in my arms for a private kiss only twice. Our children will never believe this. Nobody will believe it."

"Well, if all goes well and Lucille and Nancy come over to stay, I'll try to change our record, at least, a little,"

"Hey, wait a minute. Am I marrying a brazen woman without knowing it?"

Judith playfully mocked him. "Oh, I'm sorry. If I have given you the wrong impression, I take it all back."

"Don't you dare!" Scott said. "I believe the Lord, Himself, would want us to improve our pitiful courtship."

Chapter 17

Monday afternoon, Scott could hardly wait to bid his staff goodbye at 4 o'clock. He wanted to get ready for his big Monday night date. He laughed to himself, thinking that most fellows had Saturday night dates, but not preachers. They were too preoccupied with Sunday's messages and a multitude of pressing duties. No Saturday dating.

The first thing he planned to do when he reached home was to take a shower. *Mother would surely kid me if she were here. She used to say that if I took two showers in one day, it was a dead give-away that I had a big date planned. She would be right this time.*

He squealed to a stop in his driveway and popped open the trunk. Before taking anything inside, he opened a long, white box to check the dozen red roses, just to be sure they were all right. He had hated to leave the flowers in the car, but he had dreaded the kidding they might cause if he took them inside the church. Pleased that every rose looked as fresh as when the clerk had presented them to him, he replaced the designed tissues and closed the lid. He picked up a box of Whitman's chocolates. *I hope that salesman is right. He assured me that these are the very best chocolates on the market. I know Judith loves chocolate. And I love Judith!*

Leaving the trunk open, he took Judith's two gifts into the house before coming back for the things he had bought in Belk's for himself. The dapper young man who had waited on him had persuaded him to purchase a light grey sports jacket, black pants, a dark blue shirt and matching tie, and some new black loafers without tassels.

Even now as he looked at his new purchases, he smiled sheepishly. *I remember when my sister wanted to buy something new to wear for some occasion I would kid her. I thought what she was doing was foolish. Now, look at me! I am 28 years old and I'm acting like a teenager.*

As he showered, he belted out song after song, thankful that no one could hear him.

Lucille and Nancy came together to Hansley Haven at five o'clock. Judith flitted from room to room, pointing out plans for Granny's return. "I have been sleeping downstairs in Granny's room. That is what she wanted me to do. Now, I'll go across the hall to sleep.

Lucille looked puzzled. "I thought Brother Hansley's study was across the hall."

"I understand it used to be; but do you remember when Stan Steelman stayed here?"

"Yes. Oh, now I remember. Mr. Hansley made a bedroom out of his study so that Stan could be near him."

Lucille spread her fingers across her heart. "Oh, my, wasn't that just like Brother Hansley. Judith, you didn't get to meet him, but Philip Hansley was one of the Godliest men I have ever known."

"And handsome," Nancy added. "He and Peggy – Granny to everyone now – made the best-looking couple. And how they loved each other! You could almost feel the sparks between them."

The telephone rang and Judith picked up the receiver. "Hansley Haven," she said.

"Oh, Judith!" Mrs. Johnson said, choking back a sob.

"Mother, what is wrong?" Judith said.

"Judith, Judith, something terrible has happened. I wanted to tell you before you heard it on the news." She sobbed.

"Mother, tell me. Tell me!"

"Honey, Mike and Zack have been in a boating accident. They are not sure Mike is going to live. Zack is hurt badly, too, with three broken bones on the left side of his body."

Judith's legs gave way and she sank to the floor, crying. "Where are they, Mother?"

"They're in a hospital in Wilmington, North Carolina."

"Wilmington? Mother, what's the date?"

"June the twentieth, I think."

Judith's body was shaking. "Mother, Mother, do you realize you and I had hoped to be on that Wilmington trip with them?"

"Oh, dear me, Judith, now I remember."

Lucille knelt down beside Judith, patting her back and trying to understand the fragmented conversation. With tears in her eyes, Nancy hurried from the kitchen with a box of tissues.

For a few minutes, Judith clutched the telephone to her heart and sobbed.

At length, she spoke again to her mother. "Mom, I'm going to Wilmington. I want you to go with me. Pack some things for me and for yourself. I should be home in less than a half hour."

For the next five minutes, she tried to call Scott while she rushed around, cramming a few clothes and a makeup kit into a small suitcase. Over and over, she dialed Scott's home number and cell number with no answer. "I can't get Scott" she cried. Between sniffles, she told the two secretaries what had happened to her two dearest teacher friends. "I have to go to them. I have to. I'm sorry I can't reach Scott. He must have had some emergency. Please tell him …..tell him that Mike Moring might not make it."

Within ten minutes, Judith was speeding away, hearing Lucille and Nancy begging her to be careful.

At seven o'clock, Scott arrived at Hansley Haven and mounted the steps two at a time. He carried the cherished box of long-stemmed roses and the chocolates. Before he rang the doorbell, he straightened his jacket and glanced down at his new shoes. He laughed at himself again. *I cannot believe I'm acting like a teenager on a first date. I really must love my little Judith Johnson.*

The bell chimed. Trembling, Lucille opened the door with wide-eyed Nancy looking over her shoulder. Before either lady could say anything, Scott blurted out, "What's wrong? Why have you been crying? Where is Judith?" He pushed past them and entered the living room, calling Judith's name.

"Pastor," Lucille said, touching his arm, "Judith is not here. She's gone. She tried over and over to call you."

"I didn't get any calls," Scott said and then he remembered his loud singing in the shower. *I could not have heard a tornado.* "Why was she calling? What's wrong?"

Both women tried to tell him the news, each one adding a bit of information: Mike and some other person in a boating accident. Mike might die. Judith and her mother were supposed to be on that boat. Judith and her mother were now on the way to Wilmington, North Carolina.

Then Lucille added, "Oh, Pastor, she was really looking forward to this evening. It broke her heart to have to leave. She had new clothes and everything. She left crying."

"She had bought a really pretty dress just for you." Nancy said. It was yellow and blue, your favorite colors."

Scott shook his head as though he could not take in all the erratic information. He slumped down in an overstuffed chair and covered his eyes with his forearm. Silently he prayed, *"Father,*

I believe you picked out Judith to be my wife; but now, here again she is with Mike Moring. However, in spite of how I feel about Mike, I do pray, if it be your will, that you will bless him and spare his life.. Give the doctors wisdom. And, please, bless and protect Judith and her mother as they travel. I love you, Lord."

Slowly, he lowered his arm and looked across the room where Lucille and Nancy sat with their heads bowed as though they knew he was praying. On purpose, he made a little noise getting up.

Lucille opened her eyes and glanced at Scott. "Oh my, Pastor," she exclaimed, "you bought something new for tonight, too! How I wish Judith could see you. She would like your jacket and matching shirt and tie." Tears filled her eyes as she lowered her voice, "I'm sorry you two are not going to have the special evening both of you had worked so very hard to plan."

Scott smiled at his loyal secretary and said, "The Lord willing, we will have years of special evenings once we are married." He thought, *I only wish I knew when that would be.*

After pacing throughout the lower portion of the house, Scott finally ascended the steps and rambled around upstairs. Lucille and Nancy sat quietly, waiting and praying. When, at length, he came back down, he circled the long dining room table twice, absently-mindedly rubbing his hand over the polished surface. All the time, he was silently talking with the Lord and waiting for His leadership.

He pulled up a straight chair and sat facing the two secretaries. "This is what I'm going to do. I'm going to stay here at the Hansley Haven tonight. I need the blessing of this place upon me. I'll sleep downstairs in Granny's room. You, two, are upstairs, aren't you? The women nodded.

"I've checked my calendar. I have only one major appointment tomorrow. I'm going to ask you to re-schedule my meeting with Mr. Smith. I'm sure he will understand. I plan to go to Wilmington early tomorrow morning. I think Judith might need me there."

Secretaries Lucille and Nancy agreed.

While traveling, Judith and her mother had filled an empty Wal-Mart bag with soggy tissues as they sped down I-40. The traffic was minimal, only a car or semi-truck every now and then. Judith was thankful; for, at times, tears blurred her vision. Although she was usually a good driver, mindful to stay close to the speed limit, at times she glanced down to see the speedometer topping 80 miles an hour.

"Slow down, honey," her mother would whisper.

Both Judith and her mother had failed to keep a careful watch, however, for suddenly, they heard the dreaded, police-car siren and glanced into the rear-view mirror to spot flashing blue lights tailing them. Moaning, Judith pulled over to the side.

A middle-aged officer approached the car and asked to see Judith's license. As he flashed a light upon the card and then back upon her, he noted her puffed eyes and wet cheeks. "What's wrong, young lady? I stopped you because you were exceeding the speed limit. Is there a reason for your hurry?"

Judith looked up, blinking the tears from her eyes. "Yes, Sir. I'm on my way to a hospital in Wilmington. Two of my closest friends have been in a boating accident. One may die." She put her hand over her mouth to stifle a sob.

The officer tucked his ticket pad away. "I read about that accident," Miss Johnson. "It's really sad. I tell you what. I'm going to give you a warning about speeding, and then I'm going to escort you to the hospital. You are about 20 minutes away."

Mrs. Johnson leaned over and whispered, "Oh, thank you, Officer. Thank you."

Judith put her head down on the steering wheel. *Thank you, Lord, for sending someone to lead me. I had no idea how to get to the hospital.*

She looked up and said, "Thank you, Sir, and God bless you."

The officer whipped into the parking area at the emergency room and hurried over to Judith's car. "Park right here, young lady. I'll see that your car is moved to the right place." He opened the door and helped Judith out while her mother exited the other side. Judith glanced at her watch. It was ten o'clock. Visiting hours were over, but she knew she had nothing to worry about; the officer was leading the way.

Entering the emergency waiting room, Judith immediately spied Mike and Zack's mothers, sitting huddled close to their husbands. Both women glanced up and quickly arose to embrace Judith - - a natural thing since during the two years she had taught with Mike Moring and Zack Matson, Judith had eaten out with both families often. The fathers stood and put their arms around the women. Judith's mother moved away and sank into a nearby chair. At the door, the officer stood, fighting off tears. He had a son the exact age of the two battered young men. It was heartbreaking to see what a drunk in a speed boat could do to innocent boaters.

The two fathers left the ladies and talked with the officer. Learning this officer had knowledge of the accident, they asked him to accompany them across the room to inform the family. They mentioned the hospital personnel had told them very little.

Mr. Matson said, "Ladies, this is Officer Harrington. He can give us information about the accident."

Officer Harrington took over and gave them a detailed report: "Prior to the time that Mike and Zack entered the inland waterway at Topsail Island, a young man in a speed boat had been spotted making bizarre maneuvers. Laughing fiendishly, he would speed directly toward another boat, swerving at the last moment to prevent a crash. A distraught boatman had called 911, screaming what had happened to him and his family. Shortly afterwards, two other frenzied calls had come in, giving the same information. Authorities were on the way to the inlet when the crazed teen headed toward Mike's boat. People saw what was happening, but no one could do anything but scream. Your boys were frantically waving the speeder away and trying to steer out of reach. Their attempt must have been taken as a dare, for the stupid kid sped straight toward the boat. At the last moment, he might have tried to swerve, but his attempt was futile. He crashed broadside into the boat.

"Thankfully, your sons were rescued immediately. Already, an ambulance was waiting and they were rushed to the hospital. By the way, that foolish young man is here in the hospital, too. When he sobered up and learned what he had done, he cried and cried and begged the doctors to let him die. It is sad what alcohol and drugs can do." He paused. "I am very sorry to have to give you this bad report."

"We understand, Officer Harrington, but we really wanted to know what happened," Mr. Matson said.

"What is the status right now? Have the doctors told you anything?" the office asked.

Mr. Moring spoke first, "We don't know exactly what is happening. A doctor came out thirty minutes ago and told us that Mike has stabilized but is still in a coma. They are setting bones for Zack now. The blow shattered Zack's left side." Instantly, Mr. Moring was sorry he had said this, for Zack's mother began to sob.

Judith shuddered and hugged the grieving mother. How could this happen to two fine men like Mike and Zack? Both teachers were making great contributions to the lives of young people. Both were Christians.

Father, I know that "all things work together for good to them that love the Lord" and I know that Mike and Zack love you. Please help me understand. Please help me trust you for something good to come from this disaster. Please bless...

At twelve o'clock, Mr. Matson spoke to Judith and her mother. "Why don't you two sweet ladies go to the hotel and try to get some sleep? The four of us will be staying here all night. As parents, we can't leave; but, maybe, tomorrow when our boys are out of danger, you could relieve us and let us rest a while."

Judith was reluctant to leave, but the four parents persuaded her that their plan was a good one. She kissed the mothers goodnight, and walked over to the officer who waited to lead them to the hotel.

Chapter 18

Judith looked at her mother lying on the queen-sized bed beside her. *Poor dear. She is exhausted. She fell asleep as soon as she pulled the covers up around her. I forget Mother is not as young as she used to be.*

Almost in a daze, she washed her face, applied a light night cream, pinned up a few curls, and brushed her teeth. Slowly, she crawled into bed, knowing that she was too keyed up to sleep. *I won't fret*, she thought. *I'll lie quietly and sort things out.*

She remembered how she had questioned how all that was happening could work out for good. *Father, forgive me. I do not want to doubt your Word. I want to believe you are in control, that You have a purpose.*

She thought of Granny in Zilford's hospital. What good could she think had come from Granny's heart attack? Judith lay, eyes open wide, and then answers began to come.

Because of Granny's illness, Judith had been living in Zilford, getting to know Scott's church family and being able to hear Scott preach three times. She had found the subject for the book she wanted to write. And even more exciting, she had become friends with Debbie Peterson.

She smiled as she remembered how that came about. It was the first Sunday morning of her stay that she had been able to go to church. She was early and sat about midway back in the sanctuary. Sunday school had been dismissed, and choir members were coming into the auditorium, putting Bibles on pews where they planned to sit when they were dismissed from the choir. Debbie flitted into the room, taking time to speak to elderly people already seated and stooping to hug a child or two. After placing her Bible and purse, she glanced up and saw Judith. Smiling, she made her way to her and said, "Hey, Judith. I'm Debbie. Since your Scott and my Caleb cannot sit with us during church, why don't you come and sit with me. I really want to get to know you. I need you to teach me some things"

Her smile was so genuine that Judith got up and moved to the third pew from the pulpit.. Since that day, she had sat with Debbie twice, and the two had talked on the phone several times. Once, in the waiting room at the hospital while Caleb Barnet was in Granny's room, Debbie had whispered, "Caleb has asked me to marry him."

Judith had hugged her and said, "What did you say?"

"Well, I was going to say that I wanted to pray about it, but he did not give me a chance to answer. He told me that He had trusted the Lord to pick out his wife for him, and he felt the Lord had done so."

Judith laughed. "Funny, isn't it? That's the way Scott planned to find his right wife. I might have dismissed his idea as naïve, but I happen to know that Scott talks with the Lord more than any person I've ever known. He expects to get direct answers for everything."

"So does Caleb. Do you think those two men might be cut from the same piece of cloth?" They giggled. Judith liked Debbie Peterson. Strange how things had developed. She and Debbie were like cut-up sisters.

Yes, a major good thing from Granny's hospitalization was

this friendship Judith and Debbie now had. Both had always wanted a sister, and now each had one.

Scott Jacobs slept soundly at Hansley Haven, especially knowing that his Judith had slept in the same bed the night before. He arose early, saying aloud the verse he said every morning: **"This is the day which the Lord hath made; we will rejoice and be glad in it."**

He had not planned to eat breakfast before he left; but when he came out of his room, the aroma of bacon and hot biscuits drew him to the kitchen. Nancy was already pouring him a glass of orange juice and Lucille stood by with the coffee pot in hand. Scott could tell his middle-aged secretaries were enjoying pampering their pastor. He took his seat at the table and smiled his appreciation.

At 7 o'clock, he was on his way to Wilmington. He figured he could safely make the trip in less than four hours. Perhaps, he and Judith could have lunch together and he could learn what was happening with her friends. Too, he would be able to tell her the wonderful news he had planned to share with her on the evening of their spoiled, planned date.

He remembered his loud singing that had kept him from hearing the phone ring. That celebrating voice came, not only from his new clothes and upcoming date, but from the great news that Granny Hansley had led Dr. Thurman Higgins to a saving knowledge of Christ earlier that day. He could hardly wait to tell Judith how it had happened.

Both Scott and Judith knew that Granny had a burden for Dr. Higgins. As soon as she had become lucid, she had sensed that her doctor had a need. Maybe, that was a Hansley trait.

"Pastor," she had said softly, "Dr. Higgins is a sad man. He never smiles. He comes to my room often as though he wants to talk with me. Something is wrong, and I want you to pray with me that I'll be able to find out what it is."

She found out the day he came into her private room to tell her she would be able to go home in a couple days. When an attending nurse started to leave the room, Dr. Higgins said, "Nurse Mitchell, would you, please, close the door when you leave. I wish to talk with Mrs. Hansley."

"Ooops," Granny said when the door was closed. "Does that mean you have bad news for me?"

"No…no…no," the doctor assured her. "I want to talk with you about Hansley Haven.

Granny raised herself up and propped on her elbow. "Hansley Haven! What would you want to know about Hansley Haven?"

Dr. Higgins pulled a chair around so that he could sit facing Granny. "Mrs. Hansley," he said, "I have been a doctor in this hospital for over 20 years. During that time I have seen many broken people go to Hansley Haven, stay for a while, and come away whole, happy, and productive. I have always wondered what the secret was. To tell the truth, I thought I might like to go there myself."

Granny's blue eyes twinkled. "What a great idea. You and your wife must come when I get home. A stay at Hansley Haven might be just what your doctor orders." She wanted to point upward, but she didn't.

"All right. Tell me how men, women, young guys, and many young girls in trouble: all found their way into your home and came out so completely changed."

Granny silently prayed, "*Lord, help me. Give me the words to say. Speak to Dr. Higgins' heart.*"

"Dr. Higgins, do you mind if I ask you a question first?"

"Of course not."

Granny paused. "Dr. Higgins, do you believe in God?"

"Yes, I suppose I believe there is a God, but I do not know anything about him. Would you believe, Mrs. Hansley, I never went to Sunday school a day in my life. When I was around other children as a youngster, I realized I knew none of the Bible stories they talked about. I was embarrassed by my lack of knowledge, especially when a teenage boy pointed to me and laughed loudly because I did not know John 3:16. I had no idea what he was talking about."

"Do you mind if I ask why you didn't go to church as a boy?"

"That was my parents' preference."

Granny nodded without making a comment. She waited for the doctor to continue.

Dr. Higgins stood up and walked to the window and back before continuing. "I did go to church once with a girlfriend when I was a junior in college. She invited me to attend an Easter service with her. I must say that, although I was a little uneasy in a church setting, I did like the minister's message, however. He helped me understand why many people believe Jesus is the Son of God. At the end of the service, several people went down to an altar and knelt. I could not explain it, but I wanted to go, too. Of course, I didn't."

"Why did the minister say the people were coming to the altar? Do you remember?"

"Yes. He said they were coming to acknowledge publicly that they were accepting Christ as Savior."

Granny sat upright in bed. "Dr. Higgins, would you like for me to tell you how to accept Christ as your Savior?"

The doctor seemed a little startled by the question. "Can you do that?"

"Of course, I can," Granny said reaching into the drawer of her bedside table. She took out a Gideon Bible and opened it.

When she started to hand the Bible to the doctor, he said, "Now, Mrs. Hansley, I have already told you that I do not know anything about the Bible."

"That is all right," Granny said. "I'll show you. Now, look where I have the Bible open. You are in the book of Romans. You will see it says Chapter 3 and then there are numbered verses. I am going to tell you what to read."

The Doctor took the Bible with a slight smile on his face. "Okay, we'll see how this goes."

Granny said, "First, I want you to read Chapter 3, verse 23."

Dr. Higgins found the verse and glanced at Granny. "Out loud?"

"Yes, if you don't mind."

Dr. Higgins read slowly as though he was analyzing thoughts, **"For all have sinned and have come short of the glory of God."**

Ordinarily, Granny might have made a comment, but she felt led to let the Lord open the scripture for Dr. Higgins. Please read Romans 6:23.

He read aloud, **"For the wages of sin is death; but the gift of God is eternal life through Jesus Christ our Lord."**

Granny waited a few seconds. "Now, turn back to Romans, Chapter 5, verse 8." She smiled as he found the place. "Read that verse please."

Thoughtfully, Dr. Higgins read, **"But God commendeth his love toward us, in that, while we were yet sinners, Christ died for us."** He finished reading but kept studying the wording.

Granny prayed, *Father, it is evident You are in control here. I know I do not need to add anything. Bless Dr. Higgins with unusual insight.*

When Dr. Higgins looked up, Granny said, "Now, turn to Chapter 10, verse 9. In a few seconds, the doctor began reading: **"That if thou shalt confess with thy mouth the Lord Jesus, and shalt believe in thine heart that God hath raised him from the dead, though shalt be saved."** Again he stopped and pondered the wording.

Granny offered no explanation. When he lifted his eyes, she said quietly, "Read verse 13."

Dr. Higgins responded, **"For whosever shall call upon the name of the Lord shall be saved."** Granny waited.

With a gleam in his eyes, Dr. Higgins said, "Is this what I'm to do? Do I call on the Lord?" When Granny nodded, he said, "What do I say?"

For the first time, Granny felt free to say something. "Remember the verse you read about all being sinners? Tell the Lord you know you are a sinner and wish to turn from your sins. Ask Jesus to come into your heart. Ask Him to save you. Dr. Higgins, it is as easy at that!"

Dr. Higgins bowed his head and began to pray. His body shook with muted sobs as he talked with the Lord. Almost immediately, he began to call Him "Father" and to thank Him for saving him.

Granny lay back upon her pillow and cried for joy.

There was a light rap on the door, and Dr. Higgins wiped his eyes before saying, "Come in."

A nurse entered the room, carrying a tray of medicines. "I'm sorry to bother you," she said as she walked to the bedside.

"Think nothing of it, Nurse Matthews," Dr. Higgins said. "I'm glad you are here. You will be the first to know that I have just accepted Christ as my Savior. You see, my dear, you are not the only one who has profited by the Hansley ministry."

He winked at Granny. "I remember when this young lady was a resident at Hansley Haven.

Granny reached for the nurse's hand and squeezed it. She remembered, too.

Scott was picturing again the unusual conversion Granny had reported earlier when he entered Wilmington Hospital's parking lot. After circling three lanes, he found a spot and bounded from the car. He was in a hurry to see Judith, his Judith. He wanted to hold her in his arms (if that was possible), to tell her how much he loved her, and to tell her about Dr. Higgins' decision. He knew she and Granny had been praying for the doctor.

At the information desk, he received directions to the intensive care unit. He pushed through double doors and started a long trek down a maze of polished hallways. When he saw the waiting room sign, he slowed his pace, adjusting his tie and straightening his coat. It seemed ages since he had seen Judith and he wanted to look as nice as possible.

He entered the waiting room and searched for the blonde head he loved. He spotted Judith just as she arose from a seat near the window. He headed her way and softly called her name. She turned. Her eyes brightened even as tears welled up. She ran to him, put her arms around his neck and rested her head upon his chest.

"Oh, Scott, I am so very glad you're here." she whispered.

"I'm glad I'm here, too," he said, brushing his lips against her hair." Glancing over her head, he saw two middle-aged couples walking together toward them. *These must be the parents. How will they receive me? Did they, like Judith's teacher friends, expect one of their sons to marry Judith? Will they resent me?*

"Judith," he said, "I believe your friends' parents are headed this way. I have never met them, you know"

Immediately, Judith turned and, holding Scott's hand, met the Morings and the Matsons half way.

"Mr. and Mrs. Moring" she said, indicating the first couple," and Mr. and Mrs. Matson," indicating the other, "this is my fiancé, Dr. Scott Jacobs."

The two older men stepped forward and shook Scott's hand. "Thank you so much for coming," Mr. Moring said.

Mr. Matson added, "We would appreciate your praying for our boys. They are having a rough time."

"I'm so very sorry," Scott said. "My staff and I have been praying for Mike and Zack ever since we heard the awful news."

The wives moved forward and extended their hands, greeting Scott warmly. Judith's mother, who had stood quietly by, slipped to Scott's side and touched his elbow. "Hi, Pastor Jacobs," she whispered. "I'm glad you're here. Judith has needed you."

He grinned down at Mrs. Johnson. "You'll never know how much I have needed your little girl. I need her every day," he whispered

Scott kept vigil with the two families until midnight. Once, he had been allowed to go in to pray for each young man. He was deeply concerned when he noted Mike's pallid skin, his sunken eyes, and all the wires and tubes connected to his body. He noted that a doctor or nurse was constantly by the comatose victim, administering a procedure or adjusting some equipment.

He stood by the bed the minute he and Mike were alone and touched Mike's clammy hand. He prayed quietly, *"Dear Lord, this is Mike Moring. I bring him before you. He is your child. His parents have told me that he has loved you since he was a little boy. Would you, please, remember his love for you. Please be near him now. Touch his body if it can be your will. Lift him up so that he may continue to serve you."*

He could not be sure, but he felt that Mike moved his hand slightly.

Before he entered Zack's room a while later, Judith pulled him slightly down to whisper into his ear. "Look inside Zack's room. There are always two or three nurses there. It is not often they get to care for such a handsome, eligible man."

Scott hated her wording, but he looked down and smiled.

Judith went on to explain, "Zack has been awake, free from pain, ever since his ribs were taped and his arm and leg set. He has lain there, highly medicated, marveling at the attention he is getting. He does not know what condition Mike is in. He has no worries."

"That is good," Scott said as he headed into the room to pray for another young man who had made, and could still make, him jealous.

Chapter 19

Judith was waiting by the door when he returned from Zack's room. Facing Scott but keeping her back to the waiting room, she said, "Scott, see the couple seated on the sofa?" She waited a second. "They are Mr. and Mrs. Norwood, the parents of the young boy who caused the wreck. Look at them. They are heartbroken." Scott shook his head sadly. The man and woman sat, leaning against each other, heads bent to their chests, swollen eyes closed.

"How's their son? Scott asked.

"Johnny has some injuries, but the doctors think he will be all right if he ceases begging to die."

"Begging to die?"

"Yes. When he learned what he had done, he wanted to die."

Scott turned his head. "Judith, let's see if we can find a secluded spot to pray with his parents. Then, I'll go in and have prayer with Johnny."

"Please do; but before you do, I want to tell you why his parents are having such a hard time. You see, Johnny has never been in any kind of trouble. He has always been a model child, an honor student. As a matter of fact, he has had two offers of full-time scholarships to prestigious colleges this fall. He has just accepted one up north."

Glancing across the room, Judith placed her hand over her heart as though hurting for the Norwoods. "Here's the thing that is difficult to understand," she said, "Johnny has no reputation of drinking or taking drugs; and yet, tests have revealed huge amounts of both in his system."

Judith quit speaking, for two uniformed officers entered the room and went to Mr. and Mrs. Norwood. They spoke quietly to the couple and then walked with them out into the hall. Scott and Judith gazed at each other with deep concern.

In minutes, one officer returned and approached Scott and Judith. "Excuse me," he said. "I understand from Mrs. Norwood that you two are here with the Moring and Matson families."

"Yes, we are," Scott said. "I'm Scott Jacobs, a minister friend, and this is Miss Johnson who has taught with Mike and Zack for two years. Judith nodded, forcing a smile.

"I'm Officer Rex Carter. "I'm here to inform the Norwoods what happened to their son. You see, two young men came into our station two hours ago and confessed to their part in what, they had planned, to be no more than a mere prank. Since Mike and Zack's parents are out having dinner, the Norwoods are wondering if you would like to hear the latest report. May I say, I think it would be an excellent idea. When the young men's parents return from the restaurant, they may need the kind of report and support you, two, can give them, even if we are still here. You understand, all of these parents are very distraught."

When Scott gave consent, Officer Carter tilted his head toward the door, and another officer stepped inside. Silently, he ushered the Norwoods into the room and led them to a round table in the far corner of the room. Scott and Judith were led to the same table.

Before taking a seat, Judith picked up a box of tissues to place on the table. She knew whatever news to be reported would be soul-wrenching for the grieving parents.

The older officer said, "Mr. and Mrs. Norwood, we know how you have repeatedly questioned the reported actions of your son. I am happy to tell you that your confidence in your Johnny was not misplaced. We now have proof that what Johnny Norwood did was not his fault."

Mrs. Norwood clasped both hands over her mouth and stifled sobs. Her husband slipped closer to her and put his arm around her shoulders.

The officer cleared his throat and continued: "Johnny was out with four of his football teammates. They were celebrating finishing high school as state champions.

"One of the players – Philip Goss, I think his name was – came up with an idea when Johnny went to the restroom. The boys decided to get Johnny drunk and to leave him on his dad's speedboat where he would wake up alone the next morning.

"The plan started. After they had ridden around awhile, Philip stopped by his house and came out with two bottles of Vodka under his coat. They then went by two more homes, and let the other guys raid their parents' medicine cabinets for tranquilizers. Johnny had no idea what they were doing.'

The officer stopped to check his notes. "They, then, went to Bill Vinton's home and began watching a video called "Chicken Fear." Perhaps, you have heard of this video; it's an old one that has long caused concern among law officers and parents. We have seen many tragedies as a result of this exciting, but dangerous, video."

When the officer noted that all of them raised quizzical eyebrows, shook their heads or shrugged their shoulders, he gave a quick synopsis: "The film shows young people doing dangerous things on a dare. For instance, two cars race toward each other, head on. Each driver is certain the other driver will 'chicken out' in time to avoid a collision. In the video, on the first two crazy runs, someone does chicken out; but on the third, there is a deadly crash." Here, the officer shook his head sadly, remembering such heartbreaking losses.

"Another scenario uses the speedboat scare, a driver racing toward a helpless boater, planning to turn away at the last second. This video was the one the guys wanted your son to see. They re-ran that scene over several times, 'whooping it up' when the speedboat failed to career to safety. Your son did not think the dare games were funny."

"It was then that Philip took out the Vodka and said, 'Johnny, my boy, this is your night to celebrate. You have gone all the way through high school without a single drink. We want you to change that record tonight.'

'Not on your life!' Johnny said. "I have too many good things going for me to mess things up by drinking.'

"The urging began with all four merely teasing him. When the teasing became increasingly more coercing, Johnny became uneasy; he asked Philip to take him home. The guys laughed and shoved him around a bit."

Mrs. Norwood made an audible sob. Anger filled her husband's eyes.

"Pinning him to the kitchen floor, they tried to make him drink. Someone pried his mouth open; someone steadied his head. Ben held up a funnel and said, 'Hey, look what I got from Mom's kitchen. We can funnel it in.' Johnny's struggling became a challenge to the four. Little by little they forced pills and Vodka into his system until Johnny no longer resisted. When he passed out, they carried him to the car and drove to the docks. Three of the boys had been out on the boat with Mr. Norwood and Johnny before. They knew where supplies were. Using Johnny's lock-out keys, they got a pillow and blanket and, jokingly, put him down for the night. According to Philip, they really meant Johnny no harm; they could foresee no problems." Closing his note pad, the officer said, "Philip Goss and Bill Vinton turned themselves in today, knowing that the mixture of Vodka and questionable drugs must have driven Johnny over the edge. They wanted to clear Johnny's good name."

Judith slipped onto the couch next to Mrs. Norwood and gave her a lingering hug. Without speaking, Mr. Norwood got up and walked from the room, down the hallway, and into the parking lot where he paced back and forth, gritting his teeth.

Scott watched from the window, waiting for the Lord to lead him to Mr. Norwood. *Bless him, Father. Give me the right scriptures to pass on to him when the time is right. Heal this broken heart, please, in Jesus' name. Oh, yes, dear Lord, please deliver him from temptation; for right now, I know he would like to bop Philip Goss and Bill Vinton.*

Chapter 20

At six o'clock Tuesday evening, Scott came into the waiting room and headed straight to Judith, excitement in his eyes. He dangled two keys before her and said, "Judith, my dear, I have been talking with Officer Karen. Look what he gave me! These are the keys to his ocean-front cottage at Surf City, North Carolina. No one is there this week, and he has offered the place to me. I know we can't stay overnight; but if we leave now, we will have a few hours at the beach before bedtime. We're only 40 minutes away!"

Judith listened to his long, non-stop message without speaking. Only her raised eyebrows expressed her questions.

"It is only 40 or 45 minutes, at the most, away. We don't have to take a thing. We might pick up some Kentucky Fried Chicken on the way just in case we get hungry."

His enthusiasm was contagious. Judith's eyes danced as she said, "Let's go. Let's go! Mother stayed at the hotel this evening. I'll call her and tell her what we are doing.

"You call her, and I'll go over and talk with the Morings and Matsons. I'm sure they will not mind. They will have each other as they wait, and I'll give them our phone numbers."

Like children, Scott and Judith raced up the long, wooden steps to the beach home. Although Officer Karen had called it a cottage, the structure was more like an elaborate home mounted on pylons, allowing it to tower above the shoreline. Laughing and oohing and aaahing, Judith darted from room to room, commenting on the spaciousness, the coordinated blue and yellow décor in one bedroom; the beige and browns in another; the yellow and orange in the bunk bedroom; and above all else, the breath-taking view from the glassed-in front.

Scott opened the sliding glass doors and they walked out onto the deck. In awe, the two stood gazing at God's magnificent handiwork - the seemingly endless water, water, water, stretching to a distant, faint horizon; and, from the right and left, as far down the coast as one could see.

"Ooooh, it's so beautiful!" Judith said.

"It is, isn't it?' Scott said as he moved to stand behind her and to loop his arms around her. She leaned back against him and rested her head upon his chest. Scott's heart began to beat fast; he had never held her in his arms this way. He loved her nearness to him; and yet, the sensation that swept through his body troubled him. How often had he counseled young dating couples, teaching them to avoid temptations. He thought of the scripture verses he had so very often quoted: *"Flee also youthful lusts...."* or **Make no** *provisions for the flesh."* He released his snug hold and said, "Come on. Take off your shoes. Let's go walk on the beach."

Judith laughed. "I was just getting ready to suggest that to you. Our great minds are running together." Scott wondered if she, too, had received a danger signal.

Dusk was settling, accentuating the slate-gray of the waves and the scattered white foam. Holding hands, Scott and Judith had strolled, barefooted, in the edge of the waters, for over an hour, now and then being splashed up above their rolled-up slacks.

"I love this beach," Scott said. "It seems to be so very private. Do you realize we have passed only ten or twelve people? I say, Judith, let's bring our children here someday."

Judith smiled. She loved the way the two of them were always making plans for the children they would have someday.

When it was getting dark, they returned to the Karen home, showered the sand from their feet, and went inside for their Kentucky Fried Chicken. Although they did not mention it, both were keenly aware that their cherished time together was about to end.

It crossed Scott's mind that during his undergraduate days, guys came back from weekends, bragging about sleeping with their girlfriends. He always hated their thoughtless remarks, sorry for the girls' reputations they besmirched. But now, for a fleeting second, he thought how wonderful it would be to spend even one night with Judith. He loved her so much that sometimes it hurt. *Father, help me. I love Judith Johnson with all my heart. Keep my love pure. Deliver me from temptations; and if it can be your will, let us be married soon.*

They were going from room to room, checking to see that all doors and windows were locked. In the hallway, before they turned out the last light, Scott pulled Judith to him and said, "Sweetheart, before we leave, let me have one last kiss with no audience watching to censor us or to cheer us on."

Judith grinned. "Our love life really has been a public one, hasn't it?" She tilted her head and closed her eyes as his lips pressed upon her lips. It was a long, sweet kiss with no hint of wild passion, just perfect, sweet love.

When Scott released his embrace, Judith whispered, "And now, may I request one last kiss before we leave." Scott needed no prodding. He drew her close again and kissed her tenderly.

After the kiss, Judith gave a soft sigh. "Scott, I'll always remember this special kiss."

"Good or bad?"

"Oh, very good." Judith said and, as she started out the door, added, "Honey, remind me to tell you about Maggie Hitterfeld." Laughing, Scott questioned the name.

"Yes, Maggie Hitterfeld. I'll tell you about her later."

They had ridden about one-half hour when Scott remembered. "Say, Judith, tell me about Maggie Hitterfeld."

Judith adjusted her seat belt so that she could turn slightly to face him. A grin spread across her face as she began her tale:

Maggie Hitterfeld was an elderly, retired teacher who came to our school this year to visit her old faculty friends. She had recently married, and the teachers wanted to know how she met her husband.

Maggie explained, "He and I met in the cemetery. We were both there to put flowers on our spouses' graves. We started talking and then eating out. He was 70 years old and I said to myself, 'If he kisses me and it's a wimp of a kiss, I'm not going to have anything else to do with him.' Well, he kissed me, and I tell you that kiss curled my toes!"

Scott laughed.

Judith shrank back in her seat and said demurely, "Remember, I told you I would always remember that kiss in the hallway. Did you wonder why?"

"No. Why?"

She put her hands up against her cheeks as though embarrassed. She said, "I will always remember that kiss, for it curled my toes."

Scott chuckled. "Judith Johnson," he said, "our children and I are going to love living with you."

Wednesday morning as they ate breakfast, Scott said, "Judith, I am sorry I must go home today. If we were having an ordinary prayers service this evening, Pastor Billings or Caleb could speak for me; but, unfortunately, we are having our quarterly business meeting, and I have to be there. I always chair that meeting. And, too, we have a few important issues to take care of this time. Sorry. I would much rather stay here with you."

"I would really love having you here with me," she said as she reached over and touched his hand, "but I understand."

Later, when they reached the hospital, they were greeted by elated parents who could hardly wait to share the news: Scott was awake!

Mrs. Moring's eyes filled with tears and her voice quivered as she added, "But, he can't see!"

"He can't see?" Judith said.

Mr. Moring put his arm around his wife's shoulders, "But, Dear, you must remember what the doctor said. He can't see now, but that does not mean he will never see." He looked at Judith and explained, "The doctor says that some people come out of comas in stages. He surely will gradually see perfectly."

Scott seized upon that hope. "Here, let's have prayer right now that God will give Mike complete healing, that He will restore his sight. Scott drew the group together and quietly led in prayer.

Mrs. Moring hugged the young pastor when he had finished praying and thanked him. "Now, Pastor, why don't you and Judith go in to see Mike for a few minutes?"

"If that is permissible, we would love to do so. I must leave in a short while, and I surely want to see Mike."

When they entered the room, Judith went to the bedside. She took Mike's hand and said, "Mike. This is Judith. It's about time you were waking up!"

Mike turned his head her way. "Judith, I am so glad you are here." His lips quivered. "Judith, I can't see. I can't see!"

Judith patted his hand and leaned down close to his face. "But you will see, Mike. You will see! You have been in a coma. The doctor says that waking up in stages is normal for some people." Tears ran down her cheeks as she watched Mike clinch his jaws to keep from crying.

With trembling lips, Mike spoke, unmindful that anyone else was in the room. "Judith," he said, "please don't' leave me. Please, please, promise you won't leave me. I want you here. When I get my sight back, I want your face to be the first face I see."

Startled by his request, Judith looked across at Scott who had stepped back a couple feet, a troubled expression upon his face. She slightly shook her head and then bent to put her cheek next to Mike's wet face. "I'll be here, Mike. I promise I'll be right here."

Scott cleared his throat and stepped up to the bed. "Mike," he said, "This is Pastor Scott Jacobs. I'm here, too. I'm sorry, Mike, but I need to get back to my church for a meeting. Before I leave, however, I would like to have prayer for you. Will that be all right?"

"I would appreciate that very much," Mike said softly, folding his arms across his chest. Scott laid his hand on Mike's upper arm and prayed; then he turned to Judith to say, "I'm really sorry I have to leave here at this time. I don't want to leave Mike and Zack; and, of course, I don't want to leave you. Honey, I'm sorry I have to go"

"I understand, Scott, but you are doing me a great favor. My mother really needs to go back home. Her job is pressing right at this time, and she is needed. Thank you for taking her home for me. For now, I really need to be here with my teacher friends and their parents. Too, I'm the reporter to our principal who wants to keep the faculty informed. I do hope you understand."

She turned and touched the foot of the bed. "Mike, I'm going to walk with Scott and my mother to the car, but I'll be right back. Your parents will be with you while I'm gone."

"Thank you," he murmured and turned his head away.

At the car, Judith hugged her mother and gave her a kiss on the cheek. Scott got into the driver's seat, not waiting for her to come around to his side. When she came to his door, she hesitated. Having to stoop to kiss him inside the car was almost demeaning. *What is wrong with him? He could have waited for me to tell Mother good bye.*

Quelling the angry impulse she had to simply walk away, she leaned over and said, "Good bye, Scott, I hope to be home Sunday. I do want to see Dr. Higgins be baptized." Before he could turn his face to her, she gave him a quick kiss on the cheek and moved away from the car. Scott started the motor without looking at her and backed out from his parking place.

As they rode along, Scott said, "Mrs. Johnson, do you mind if we listen to some pretty, escape music? I need to do a little thinking."

Mrs. Johnson answered, "Listen to anything you like. I like 'non-talking' myself at times."

Scott reached down and touched the Escape Station, but the stringed music had barely begun before he turned the radio off. "Mrs. Johnson, I have a little problem I need to talk with you about."

"Of course, Son."

"It's about Judith and Mike. In the room a while ago, he asked her to promise she would stay with him. He begged her, and she promised. She promised without a second's hesitation. I must tell you I experienced great fear when I saw Judith pressing her face to his face, with both of them crying. In that moment, I wondered if she was learning that she really loves Mike and that she had always loved him."

"Oh, no, Scott." Mrs. Johnson said quickly. "Judith truly loves you. I know, for I have talked with her almost every day since you two met. She has never cared for anyone the way she cares for you. It is true that she, Mike, and Zack have had a very close friendship over the last two years, but she never talked about them the way she has talked about you. I know, without a doubt in my mind, that she loves you. She believes God has brought you two together."

They sat quietly for several minutes, and then Scott turned the radio on.

Chapter 21

Scott reached Zilford in early afternoon, experiencing some of the anxieties ministers face after an absence from their flock. Had anyone needed him? Had he missed something he needed to do? Was anyone sick? Were there any more called board meetings?

His concerns were allayed the minute he entered the church, however, for Lucille and Nancy beamed as they shared several items of good news. He listened as they rattled off reports, silently thanking the Lord for these two great workers God had given him.

Granny Hansley was going home Thursday afternoon and arrangements had been made for different ladies to stay with her each day. Secretaries Lucille and Nancy were still staying at the Hansley Haven each evening. *God bless these two women,* he thought again. *I don't know what I would do without them.*

Mrs. Hilton was in the hospital, but she vowed she was waiting for the pastor to come back before having her twins. The Caesarean delivery was scheduled for Thursday morning. *Thank you, Father, for letting me get back in time for these births.*

And the minutes of the last church business meeting and the agenda for the evening's meeting were typed and on his desk.

"Lucille and Nancy, you two are such a blessing to me. If you were 80 years old, I would give you a hug! It's a good thing you're only 39." Pastor Jacobs said. Both ladies giggled and turned red in their faces.

As they were leaving, Lucille turned and said, "Oh, yes, Pastor, your mother called. Your family is coming Friday morning and will be here for the weekend."

Early Friday morning Scott sat at his desk, his calendar and planning book before him. Every minute was claimed for the day. He anchored his elbows upon his desk and rested his bowed head into his hands. *Dear Lord, I have so very much to do today that I need to start with a sweet session with you. First, I wish to praise you for your great love, for saving me and calling me into your ministry. I love you, Father, and want to please you in all that I do.* He became silent, basking in the loving presence of the Lord.

For a long period, he called the names of his people who had specific needs. When he mentioned Paul Peeks who was burdened with a financial crisis, he claimed Philippians 4:19 for him: "**But my God shall supply all your need according to his riches in glory by Christ Jesus.** When he prayed for Dr. Higgins, he whispered aloud Ephesians 2:8: "**For by grace are ye saved through faith; and that not of yourselves: it is the gift of God.**" *Thank you, Lord, for Dr. Higgins' sweet conversion. Bless him now as he shares his faith with his family.*

He lowered his hand and picked up his notebook. *You know my plans. Please give leadership and anoint my ministry for today's tasks.*

By the time the other staff members arrived at the church, Scott had spent a quiet hour with the Lord. He prayed with his co-workers and then handed Lucille his agenda so that she would know where to reach him during the day. Then he was off!

Friday afternoon Judith was re-arranging Mike's flowers when she heard him utter her name. She turned quickly, for the sound he made was unusual. She gasped. Mike was lying there, holding his hand up before his face and wiggling his fingers. Tears were running down the side of his face. Judith hurried to his side.

"What is it, Mike? What is it? Can you see?"

He reached up and touched her face. His eyes widened with awe. "Judith, my beautiful Judith. I can almost see you clearly. It is as though a light is slowly coming on. Please don't move. Let me look at you."

Judith was crying as she reached the button to summon someone at the nurses' station.

"Yes? Is there something you need?" a voice said.

"Yes!. Yes! Mike is beginning to see. Tell his doctors. Tell his parents."

In minutes, the room was flooded with doctors and nurses. Judith wanted to slip out of the way, but Mike clutched her hand.. "Don't go, Judith," he said.

Dr. Smithfield bent over and spoke as he loosened Mike's fingers. "Okay, Son. You can let go now. Ms. Johnson is not going anywhere, but we need to check your eyes. She will be right here." He smiled up at Judith as she eased slightly back from the bed.

Later, Judith hugged Mike's parents before she hurried into the hall to make a call. She had to let Scott know.

In a quiet corner, she slipped her cell phone from her pocket and hit Scott's number.

"Scott Jacobs speaking," his deep voice said.

"Oh, Scott! Scott, Mike can see! He has just regained his sight! He can see! The doctors are with him now."

"Well, praise the Lord," Scott said. "I prayed for him this morning." He added, "I prayed for you, too."

"Thank you. Thank you, Scott. Do you know what this means? I can come home Sunday. I can see Dr. Higgins being baptized."

Scott said, "That's great news," but he thought, *Why didn't you say you could home to me?*

Rebuking himself for being childish, he said, "I'm glad you can be here to see Dr. Higgins being baptized. Granny is hoping to come to church Sunday, too. She will be happy you are back. You will be staying with her, I suppose?"

"Yes, if she has room," Judith said with a little laugh.

"She will have room for you, I'm sure." He wanted to say, "I will have room for you always"; but, for some reason, he merely said, "I'm glad you are coming home."

"I am glad, too. I can hardly wait to talk with you. I have so much to tell you."

"Good or bad?" he asked.

"Good, of course. Oh, Scott, I have missed you so. Do you know how much I love you?"

These words yanked him back from his gloom, his worrying about losing Judith to Mike. "I love you, too, Honey, and I have been miserable without you."

"I feel the same way about you. I can be in a room filled with people and feel so very lonesome for you that I could cry." Tears automatically came to her eyes.

Scott said, "Before you hang up, can you tell me some of the good news you have to share? I have a pushed schedule today and I could thrive on a bit of good news."

"Well, let me see. Do you remember the little, red-headed nurse that was forever in Zack's room?"

"You mean the one called Bonnie?"

"Yes. Well, Bonnie's father is the principal of the local high school. She brought her dad out to meet Zack, and yesterday he offered Zack a teaching position for this school year. Zack would get to teach Speech and Drama and would present two plays during the year. These are the subjects Zack always wanted to teach, but there are very few speech openings in schools."

"And, is he going to accept the position?"

"He is, and he seems very happy. He and Bonnie are really hitting it off well."

"That is good news. Want to tell me anymore good news?"

"No, dear, if you don't mind, I'll tell you when I see you. I will say that I think you will like what I have to tell you. Is that all right?"

"I guess it will have to do. Judith, I hate to say, 'goodbye,' but I have an appointment in ten minutes. I love you and can hardly wait to get you back in Zilford."

They said goodbye and, though they were miles apart, both held their cell phones in place for a few moments to keep the feeling of closeness.

Chapter 22

Judith glanced down at the dashboard clock. It was 9:00.. She had been concerned about getting to Zilford in time for the morning worship service, but she could not leave Wilmington until she saw Mike. She had to assure him that she would be praying for him and that she would always consider him to be one of her dearest friends.

"That is not what I wanted to hear you say, but I will learn to live with it," he said, gently taking her left hand and looking at her engagement ring. "I always wanted to be the person to put rings on this hand; but, I suppose, God has other plans." They laughed and she stooped to kiss his cheek before leaving.

Known for being a cautious driver, she set the cruise control only three miles above the speed limit and settled in for the four-hour drive. Since it was Sunday morning, she did not have to fight much traffic. She glanced across to the two lanes going in the opposite direction. *It looks as though more people are headed toward the beach, rather than leaving the way I'm doing.* She looked ahead at the long ribbon of road and checked her rear view mirror. Only one, semi-truck in view. "I'm counting my blessings," she said aloud. She reached over and turned on the radio, hoping to find a Christian station.

She sped by long stretches of undeveloped forest land;

scattered patches of swamps; and side roads, seemingly entering from nowhere. No historic sites. Few homes. No animals. Just highways and mile signs. She was determined to take only one break. She had to reach Zilford before 11 o'clock.

When she was only thirty miles away, she began adjusting her clothing, smoothing her skirt and checking her knitted top. She glanced at her high heel pumps that lay in the floor of the passenger side. How she wished she had her mother with her to drive now so that she could do some last-minute primping. Steering with her left hand, she sought to comb her hair and to adjust the mirror for last-minute makeup touches.

At 10:45, she swung into the church's filled parking lot, praying for a spot, and finally finding one in a far corner. Quickly, she switched shoes and gave one final look into the mirror, praying that she looked presentable. She bounded from the car and headed for the church while juggling her purse and Bible and struggling to slip on a short-sleeved jacket.

In the foyer, she smiled at a familiar usher; and as she took a program, she asked if he knew where Debbie Peterson was sitting. He glanced through the double doors and nodded. "I'll take you to her when they stand to sing," he said.

When she was ushered to the row where Debbie usually sat, Judith was surprised to see Scott's young sister, who quickly moved Bibles and pocketbooks so that she could make extra room on the pew. The service had not yet begun; so Judith was able to whisper, "I didn't know you were here,"

"We came Friday," she whispered back. "I'm glad you got here in time. This is going to be a great service. You'll see."

The organ and piano began to play and the choir filed in. After the congregation had sung one song, the associate pastor stepped to the podium. He welcomed everyone and then said, "As is the custom in Zilford's Community Church, our baptismal services are held at the beginning of our morning service. We trust your hearts will be blessed as you view your brothers and sisters in Christ following the Lord in baptism.

The baptismal curtain behind the choir opened, revealing Pastor Jacobs facing the congregation. He started to speak but, seemingly, had to stop to regain composure. "My dear friends," he said, "today we are blessed to have a very unusual, baptismal service.

He turned and extended his hand as Dr. Higgins entered the water. "This is Doctor Thurman Higgins. Sometimes we do not understand why some things happen as they do. For instance, as a church, it was hard for us to accept the fact that our beloved Granny Hansley, as we call her, had a heart attack; but God had a special reason. He was taking the Hansley Haven ministry to the hospital. There, our Lord gave Granny a burden for Dr. Higgins. She prayed for him constantly and in due time, she had the joy of leading the good doctor to a saving knowledge of Christ." There was a chorus of quiet Amens in the church. People began wiping tears from their eyes as the doctor cried openly.

"Dr. Higgins," the pastor said as he placed his arm around his shoulder, "you know that you have accepted Christ as your Savior and you are willing to make Him Lord of your life?"

The doctor nodded his head, "Absolutely," he said.

Pastor Jacobs lifted his right hand and said, "Because of your expressed faith in the saving power of the Lord Jesus Christ, I baptize you, Dr. Thurman Higgins, in the name of the Father, and the Son and the Holy Ghost." He lowered the older man into the water. "Buried with Him in death, now risen to newness in life." He lifted the doctor and the two men embraced for sacred moments. Then, the pastor did an unusual thing; he stepped backward and allowed Dr. Higgins to face the congregation:

"I asked Dr. Jacobs if I might have this opportunity to speak to you. For over 25 years I have been a cardiologist at the Zilford Hospital. My two children have gone to school with your children, and my wife has served on committees with many of you ladies; yet there are things you do not know about me or my family.

"I was brought up by hardworking, professional parents; but, unfortunately, my parents were indifferent to teachings about God. No one in our family attended church. As a youngster, I saw my friends going to what they called Sunday school and I wanted to go but knew that I couldn't. In high school, I envied young people my age when I saw them going to church. I felt an emptiness in my life; but out of respect for my parents, I never mentioned my concerns.

"In later years, I really began to know I was missing something, especially, when I met unhappy, often destitute people who went to Hansley Haven and eventually came away so very different. I witnessed changed lives, a thing I could not explain.

"I read in the paper when Mr. Hansley died and regretted that I had not met him. I must say, I was thankful when Mrs. Hansley became my patient. I thought God was giving me another chance to understand what happens when people become Christians.

"The pastor says that Granny (May I call her that, too?) was praying for me. That would explain why I felt drawn to her room. I had to talk with her, sometimes two or three times a day.

"Later, I will tell you how she led me to Christ, but now I want to tell you what a joy filled my life the moment I asked Christ to come into my life. " The doctor's face beamed. "I experienced unexplainable peace and happiness. I wanted to tell everyone what had happened to me. I knew immediately that I had to take the message to my wife and my two children.

"I went to the book store and bought four Bibles and had

our names engraved on the covers. In each Bible, I marked the scriptures that Granny had shown to me. I called my son and my daughter and asked them to come home.

"When they arrived, I gave each a Bible; and my wife, my children and I sat at our dining room table. There, I shared with them what had taken place in my life. I shared with them the marked scriptures." He closed his eyes and tried to hold back tears. "I apologized to my family for leaving out all spiritual aspects in our lives. I begged them to forgive me.

"Before we left the table that evening, my wife and children accepted Christ as their Savior, and I am happy to tell you that Dr. Jacobs is now going to baptize all three of them." His head rested upon his chest and tears flowed down his cheeks as the pastor moved forward and extended his hand to someone entering the pool.

Mrs. Higgins came first. "I baptize you, my sister, Helen Higgins, in the name of the Father and the Son and the Holy Ghost."

The 21-year-old son followed. "I baptize you my brother, Thurman Higgins, Jr., in the name of the Father and the Son and the Holy Ghost."

To nineteen-year-old Annette, he said, "I baptize you my sister, Annette Higgins, in the name of the Father and the Son and the Holy Ghost."

Suddenly Granny Hansley stood and clapped her little hands, saying, "Well, glory!"

In a moment, the entire congregation stood and applauded. The pastor lifted his right hand and said, "Glory be to the Father and the Son and the Holy Ghost."

The Minister of Music stepped to the podium and said, "While you are standing, let's sing together, "Jesus Saves."

The baptistery curtain closed as the Higgins family put their arms around each other in a huddle, their heads bowed together.

Chapter 23

In the sanctuary, the Music Minister stepped forward to lead the hymn the pastor had suggested. Sopranos, altos, tenors, basses, and "whatever" voices blended together in singing:

"We have heard the joyful sound, Jesus saves! Jesus saves!

Spread the tidings all around: Jesus saves! Jesus saves!

Bear the news to every land, Climb the steeps and cross the waves;

Onward! 'tis our Lord's command: Jesus saves! Jesus Saves!"

When the last stanza was almost ended, Pastor Jacobs entered the sanctuary followed by the Higgins Family. The pastor mounted the steps to the platform as an usher seated Dr. Higgins' family on the front pew.

On cue, the choir arose and presented a grand arrangement of "How Great Thou Art." They were being seated when a man stood in the audience and said, " Pastor, may I say something?"

"Of course, Brother Swartz," Scott said with an inward hesitation. He was remembering the cautions his professors had given with regards to unexpected requests to speak during services, but he knew Abe Swartz and had respect for the elderly man's judgment. "Would you like to come to the pulpit, or would you rather a microphone be taken to you?"

Abe was already exiting his pew. "I'll come there if you don't mind."

In a few moments, he stood facing the congregation. "For the past year, I have been a member of Zilford's Community Church. Some of you know that I am Jewish. I came from a very orthodox Jewish family. All my life, I had attended synagogues; and although I had some Gentile friends, I had never been inside a Christian church.

"It often bothered me that you Christians would accept a Jewish man as Messiah. I wanted to hear your reasons for doing this, but I never asked anyone; that is, until I met Pastor Jacobs.

"As a lawyer, I had drawn up many papers for your church during your building projects. I was in the process of completing a file on your latest expansion when Scott Jacobs became your pastor. I had met with him only two times before he said, "Mr. Swartz, I understand you are Jewish. You know that, as a protestant minister, I believe that Jesus Christ is the promised, Jewish Messiah, the Savior of the world. If you would ever care to discuss it, I would like to tell you why I believe this.

"I called him the next day and asked if he could come to my office. I want you people to know it wasn't that I was too cheap to take him out to lunch; I just wanted privacy for our meeting." The congregation laughed, knowing Mr. Swartz always joked about being "tight."

"After that first meeting, he and I spent hours together with Pastor Jacobs pointing out scriptures starting in the Pentateuch and laced through the Old Testament . Eventually, my eyes were opened. I grasped the significance of the prophecies. I believed!

"Praise the Lord, on a Saturday evening, I knelt by a chair in the pastor's kitchen and accepted Jesus Christ as my Savior, my Redeemer, my Messiah." He raised his hand in praise and then tuned to hug the pastor.

"Pastor Jacobs had taught me two verses of scripture. John 1: 11 and 12 says, *'He came unto his own, and his own received him not. But as many as received him to them gave He power to become the sons of god, even to them that believe on his name.'* "I am happy today for I am now a true son of God**.**" He raised his hand in praise and then turned to hug the pastor.

A woman stood and said softly, "Pastor, may I say something?" The momentary uncertainty that Scott felt was quelled immediately by an inner voice that seemed to say, "Do not fear, my son; I am in control."

The pastor turned to Caleb and said, "Take her a mike, Brother Caleb," and then added, "Mrs. Brown, you may testify where you are. I am sending you a microphone."

Mrs. Brown's testimony was different from Dr. Higgins' or Mr. Swartz's. With few words, she told how she had been brought up in a good church; but as a teenager, she rebelled, feeling angry that she had been "made" to go to church. When she went away to college, she quit attending church. She mocked her former beliefs. During her junior year, however, she found that the longer she stayed away from church and the more she transgressed biblical teachings, the more unhappy she became. She experienced an emptiness she had never known. On her twentieth birthday, tearfully, she knelt in her dorm room alone and prayed the repentant words of David in Psalm 51:12, *"Restore unto me the joy of thy salvation...."*

After two or three others had stood to speak, each giving scriptures they had claimed, a tall, teenage boy with shaggy, curly hair stood. He was handed a microphone. Turning so that he could face everyone, he said. "My name is Bart Harington. I am 18 years old, and this is the first time in my life that I have ever been inside a church. I'm here today only because a teen who works with me in the Wal-Mart stockroom invited me." He grinned. "I really came because he asked me to eat lunch at his home afterward." There was a titter of laughter.

"I cannot explain this, and I do not know a single scripture to quote to you, but I believe the Lord has spoken to my heart today." His lips began to quiver and tears formed in his eyes. He straightened up and said, "Here and now, I want to accept Christ as my Savior as these people have testified they did."

He looked at the pastor. "Would that be possible, Preacher? Could I do that now?"

Before Pastor Jacobs could finish saying, "Yes, Son," Caleb had his arm around the young man, smiling as he led him to the altar. With no music being played and no invitation being given, several teens and two adults made their way to the altar.

Scott stood behind the pulpit and said, "Ladies and gentlemen, I had a message for today, but I think the Lord and our friends have preached it for me."

When the service ended, Scott stopped at Judith's pew and said "Come and stand with me at the door this morning."

Baffled but pleased, Judith picked up her purse and Bible and slipped out into the aisle. Scott offered the crook of his arm and led her to the door. Before the congregation was dismissed by the assistant pastor and the last prayer prayed, Scott whispered, "I want people to start thinking of you as my wife."

As people began to file out, often the pastor said, "This is Judith, my fiancée." Too many times for Judith's comfort, the reply was, "Have you set the date yet?"

"Not yet, but soon," Scott said.

When there was a lull in the line, Scott said, "We're having lunch at Granny's house today." Judith started to protest. She had already being worrying about Granny's overdoing it. "Don't' worry," Scott said. "The meal has been catered and, besides, Lucille and Nancy have everything under control."

"Who will be eating with us?" Judith asked, glancing to see if anyone was approaching.

"You and your mom, my family, and the Higgins Family."

"Wow" was all that Judith could say before another family exited.

Chapter 24

"This Sunday has been simply awesome!" Judith said as she gazed at the long mahogany table bedecked with lighted candelabras, linen placemats, and Granny's best china and crystal. She noted decorative place cards to assist in the seating arrangement.

Granny was seated at the head of the table. To her right, Scott came first, then Judith, her mother, and the rest of the Jacobs family. To her left, Dr. Higgins came first with his wife and children following. A few people she had seen in church were seated at the other end of the table. Lucille and Nancy were seated next to them. Judith was happy to see that the caterers would be serving the meal, a thing she assumed they were accustomed to doing in Hansley Haven since they moved about with such ease and often bent to speak to Secretaries Lucille and Nancy.

After a lot of "ooohing" and "aaahing" over the sumptuous meal and happy, upbeat conversation all around the table, Granny pushed back slightly and said, "Okay, now, Children, I want all of you to go out into the backyard and play while our caterers clear the table. Stretch your legs a bit and enjoy this beautiful weather." Her request was as natural as a parent might have given to her family.

Smiling, although quite surprised by the backyard request, the guests rose and were led by Scott down a narrow hall which Judith had not noticed before. He opened a wide, wooden door, revealing a huge glassed-in room filled with cream-and-green, cushioned, white Wicker furniture; colorful Oriental rugs; and vibrant, blooming live plants. Soft sunlight filtered through the white blinds and gauze-like curtains, creating a tranquil atmosphere.

"This room is one of my favorites," Scott said to Dr, Higgins. A man can sit and have real communion with the Lord here."

Dr. Higgins nodded and smiled. "Think you and I could study together here sometime?"

"Absolutely. To tell the truth, I was planning to suggest that to you after I asked Granny's permission, but I'm sure she will be pleased."

Scott crossed the room and opened the outside door. Everyone inched forward, eager to see if there were other surprises. They stepped out on a railed-in porch that ran across the width of the house. In the center, curved steps led down into the yard; however, no one descended the steps. All stood looking down upon a tiny fantasy park with trellises, flowering bushes, fragrant roses, decorative fountains, blossoming plants, and swings and benches.

A tall fence, landscaped with hedges, encased the yard. From the outside, Judith previously had noticed this tall fence when she circled the block to Granny's house, but she had not pictured the Hansley property on the other side. The neatly clipped hedges that adorned the outer wooden fences surrounding the Hansley grounds provided a pleasant privacy wall.

Lucille slipped to Judith's side and said, "When I lived here, this yard was my favorite spot."

Hiding her surprise that Lucille had once been a Hansley

Haven resident, Judith answered quickly, "I can surely see why. It is so very peaceful here."

Lucille nodded and then pointed to a wooden swing beneath a trellis of roses. "That was my special seat. I could swing and think and pray."

"I liked that spot, too," Judith heard Mr. Paul Summerfield say as he moved closer.

Judith turned to look at the chairman of the deacon board and whispered, "Did you live here, too?"

"I surely did, Miss Johnson, for a few years. You see, someone dropped me off here when I was less than a year old."

He took a picture from his billfold and passed it to Judith." I was left in a baby's car seat with this picture pinned to my blanket" He smiled. "Look on the back. You'll see my biography."

Judith gazed at a picture of a smiling, beautiful baby, wearing blue pajamas with little, elf-like footies. After she had studied the picture, she turned to the back to read aloud, "Birth Date: July 9, 1956."

"And that's it. Not much of a biography, is it?" Paul Summerfield said, smiling and taking back his picture. "The Hansleys tried to find more information but never could. In true Hansley style, they took me in and cared for me until I was four years old. That's when Peter and Marcia Summerfield adopted me. For the past 32 years, I've had wonderful parents, and I love them dearly. Now, let me assure you," he said in a quiet voice while glancing around, " I love my adoptive parents and they love me, but sometimes I wonder about my birth parents. I wish I could find them. Ever since I was a teenager, Mom and Dad have always told me that they do not care if, ever, I feel the need to seek out my true parents. They know we Summerfields love each other as a family and nothing can change that."

Judith could not find words to say, but she touched the

deacon's forearm and gave a gentle pat. She had started to ask a question when Scott bustled up to her side to say, "Okay, friends, enough chit-chat. Let's go into the yard."

Paul Summerfield grinned and said, "Good idea, Pastor. I've monopolized this conversation long enough."

Hooking Judith's arm in the crook of his elbow, Scott said, "You don't know this lady, Brother Paul. She's the best listener in the world. She'd keep you talking all day. As a matter of fact, I'm marrying her so that I'll always have a sounding board."

Laughing as they descended the steps, Judith heard Nancy say, "Paul, where's your lovely wife today?'

He answered, "Little Bobby had an upset stomach and Emily had to stay with him."

"I'm sorry. Would you like for me to take food over to them?'

"Yes, Ms. Nancy. That would be great."

Judith followed Scott, whispering, "Let's go sit in that swing under the trellis."

"How did you know? That was my intended destination," he said, leading her across the lawn. Once seated, he said, "I like this area. Here, we can talk. Remember, you told me you had some good news to tell me, and you haven't told me yet."

She laughed softly. "Oh my, so much has been going on that I forgot."

Childlike, Scott had used his long legs to pump the swing backward and forward a few times before Judith said, "Before I tell you, please explain how Granny can keep this gorgeous yard."

"Oh, Granny doesn't do that. The former residents of the Haven come over and keep everything in tip-top shape. They have keys to the big gate at the side entrance and they come and go as they please. Sometimes, they come to sit and meditate or visit with other past residents. Those who live far away often send money for the upkeep."

Judith sat quietly for a while before speaking. "The Hansleys really had a ministry here, didn't they?"

"They did, and they never wanted any praise for anything they did. That was one thing that made them so very special." He touched Judith's chin with his finger and turned her head to face him. "Now, enough of the Hansley's attributes. You have some news for me."

Judith turned in the swing. Suddenly, mindful that her knees were touching Scott's leg, she moved back, surprised at the tingle she felt just being near him, even with people milling all around.

"Wipe that impish grin off your face and tell me what you have to say," Scott said.

"Okay. I will. It may be hard for you to believe, but you are now looking at this year's new eleventh- grade English teacher at Zilford High School!"

Scott's jaw dropped. For a moment, he was speechless. "You're not kidding? You mean it? You're going to be teaching right here in Zilford this year?"

"Yes, yes, yes! I went to see your principal while Granny was in the hospital and he called me on my cell phone when I was in Wilmington."

Scott asked, "Does anybody else know?"

"No. I wanted to tell you first."

Scott stood and called out in an authoritative voice, "Attention, everybody. Attention!"

When everyone was silent, he announced, "I have just learned that Judith Johnson, excuse me – soon to be Judith Jacobs - is going to be teaching in Zilford High School this coming year." He turned to Judith, pulled her to her feet and said loudly, "Do you know what that means?"

Judith faltered. "I'm not sure what you are talking about. What does it mean?"

"It means you and I can set the date! We can get married! You have to live somewhere, and I surely would like to have you live at my place; and, I'm sure these ladies who have felt compelled to feed me, would be glad to have you take over." Everyone laughed.

Judith blushed, but she whispered, "That is what I would like to do."

Lucille came out onto the porch and called, "Pastor. Pastor, Granny would like for you and Judith to come in for a few moments."

Judith and Scott raised their eyebrows and slightly shrugged their shoulders but headed for the house immediately. They found Granny still sitting at the head of the polished mahogany table. Everything had been cleared away except for a full place setting of Granny's elegant, gold-rimmed, bone china and a few special serving plates.

"Sit," she said, motioning to either side of her. She then looked at Judith. "You know, Judith, when I thought I heard the rustling of angel wings, I sent word that I wanted to see you; but then I got better and figured that what I had to tell you could wait a while longer. I bet you have wondered why I wanted to see you, haven't you?"

"Yes, Granny, I have; but I knew you would tell me if you still had something you wanted me to know."

Granny waved her arms across the exquisite china. "This is it," she said. "This is my miracle china. Everybody raves over it. There are over 24 full place settings and many, many extra pieces like serving bowls, platters, pitchers, gravy bowls, and so on. My great grandmother brought the first 12-place settings from England and my extended family has added the rest."

Scott said, "Excuse me, Granny, but why do you call this your "miracle" china?"

Granny chuckled. "I can explain that! For over 25 years, this china has been used in the Hansley Haven household, serving hundreds of hungry eaters, including children; and yet, not one, single piece has ever been broken or even chipped. Now, if that is not a miracle, there will never be one in anybody's kitchen!"

Scott and Judith both thought of their bouts with broken glasses and dishes and nodded in agreement.

"So, this is what I wanted to tell you, Judith. As a minister's wife, you have many years stretched out before you to feed the masses; so, I want to will my miracle china to you and your ministry with God's blessings upon it."

Tears rushed to Judith's eyes as she slipped from her chair, bent over, and hugged Granny, smothering her with kisses and "thank-you."

Scott got up and kissed Granny's forehead. "I'll be enjoying your beautiful china, too, Granny, and I promise I'll try to keep your beloved dishes, safe and unbroken if possible, always in God's service."

"I know you will, Son; and as you and I have already privately noted, Hansley Haven will eventually be in your hands. I have stipulated this in my will. It may be that you and Judith will want all those children you, two, are planning to have to grow up here in Hansley Haven. In time, you may have to make changes as your family grows. I've already talked with the deacons about that. They are taking care of details."

Judith did not ask any questions, but she smiled up at Scott, thinking of a house full of children playing in the fantasy-land backyard and eating at the huge polished table. Her thankful heart breathed a prayer: *Thank you, Heavenly Father, for being so very good to us. Thank you for your promise in Philippians 4:19: "**But my God shall supply all your need according to his riches in glory by Christ Jesus.**" Ahead of time, thank you, dear Lord, for our upcoming ministry in Hansley Haven. May you find us faithful.*

Chapter 25

Monday morning, Judith waited until the day nurse arrived to stay with Granny; then she slipped out quietly to run a few errands. Her first stop was at Zilford's only drug store which was a good, Monday-morning meeting place for some people.

The pharmacist had drawn up plans for his building to include middle-of-the-floor space for wrought-iron tables with glass tops and fancy iron chairs reminiscent of those in early American drug stores. For a modern touch, he had installed four, leather cushioned booths. His wife's food specialty was freshly brewed coffee, homemade muffins, and sticky buns: all favorites for businessmen.

Before taking a seat, Judith browsed the card selection, a thing she always did automatically. She picked out a sentimental card with swirls of hearts blending into each other and a cute little verse that read:

You know that I love you
By things I do and say.
You know that I need you
So say, "I do" and stay.

She paid for the card and took coffee and a sticky bun to a cushioned booth.

Slipping into her seat, she did not see Scott when he entered and went back to the card rack. She did not see him until he stopped by her booth and said, "I say, Judith Johnson, we're going to have to stop meeting like this."

She looked up, eyes sparkling.

He glanced down at the flat envelope in which her card had been placed.

Sliding into the booth, he said, "Let me see the card you bought."

Judith removed the card and opened it. Grinning, Scott held up the card he had selected. They both laughed, seeing they had purchased the same cards.

"This just shows we are meant to be together," he said. "Let's set the date for our marriage right now. Judith Johnson, WHEN will you marry me?"

Judith rolled her eyes. "One month from today," she said, placing her hands over her heart. The twentieth of July!

Scott reached into his jacket and took out his appointment book. "Good. The twentieth and that is on a Saturday. That is perfect." He wrote in his book.

Judith reached over and turned the little, leather book so that she could see the note. She loved the meticulous way Scott recorded all events. She laughed aloud when she saw the neatly-printing wording: "God is answering my prayers. Judith to become my wife." He had written the word, "time" and three question marks.

A puzzled look crossed his face. "Judith, how can you say one month from today? I thought all women say it takes a year to plan a wedding."

"It does for most people," Judith said, reaching over to take a large, white satin book from the shopping bag at her side, "but not if you know the right people." She opened the cover of the book and pointed to a big picture of Granny, her mother, his mother, Lucille, and Nancy.

She closed the book again and showed him the title of the book, "The Perfect Wedding Planner."

Eyes gleaming, she explained, "While I was in Wilmington, Granny got our mothers and your secretaries together and, with their heads put together, they planned every detail of our wedding, even our honeymoon. Read it, Honey. You will see they chose the very persons you and I wanted in our wedding, and my mother selected the bridesmaids' dresses that I love. Of course, I am going to wear Mother's wedding gown; so that was no problem.

"They have booked the church, the easiest part, and they have contacted Dr. Hudson, your beloved professor, to perform the ceremony. Lucille and Nancy have the flowers and catering checked out. And all you have to do is buy my wedding band and get fitted for your tux."

"Sweetheart," Scott said, shaking his head in disbelief, "how could they do all this without my knowing it?"

"While you were getting up that wonderful sermon that you did not get to deliver, they were meeting at Granny's house, working out details."

Scott took the card he had just purchased and with his pen he wrote the current date and beneath it two straight lines. Next he wrote the July date and two more lines. Under the June date, he signed his name, Scott Bernard Jacobs and requested Judith to sign her name, Judith Kay Johnson, beneath his. Glancing around, Scott noted he knew every person in the room. To Judith's amazement, he stood, got attention, and made an announcement.

"Friends," he said, "I'm happy to announce that in one month, this lovely lady and I are going to have the privilege to sign our names, Dr. and Mrs. Scott Jacobs. You are all invited to our wedding. Remember, you were in the room with us when

I finally got her to pin down a date." Everyone had stopped all activity to hear the announcement. Now, they applauded. Scott smiled and sat down. He liked living where everybody could know everybody.

He took the two cards they had bought earlier and said to Judith, "Put our two cards in that planning book. Our kids will get a kick out of both cards someday."

They both laughed, but Scott stopped. "Judith, you said they worked out our honeymoon. Do you mind telling me where we are going on our honeymoon?"

"To Officer Karen's ocean-front home in Surf City! Isn't that great?"

Scott went to the counter and called to the pharmacist. "Hey, Doc, could you and your wife come out here a minute, please?"

He spoke to the other customers, calling them by name. I am happy to share with you people that Judith Johnson is going to become my wife one month from today. We want you to be our honored guests. Do you know that I have wanted to marry this girl since the first time I saw her? I thought the day would never come, and now it is just around the corner."

"And to think, it all started when we bought the right card!" Judith said, holding two cards up.

Scott looked at his friends. "Wait a minute. I'm the preacher and I can say, 'You can now kiss the bride-to- be.'" If you do not mind, he said and pulled Judith to him and gave her a light, sweet kiss.

When Judith lowered her head, Scott whispered, "Why are you blushing over that little peck of a kiss?"

In cryptic language, she said quietly, "I was just identifying with Maggie Hitterfeld. My toes, you know."

They both laughed. All was well. Neither had forebodings of what was to come.

Chapter 26

June was speeding by with Granny busy showing Judith every nook and cranny in the Hansley Haven. Each room burst forth with happy color schemes and promises.

"Now, it's possible for you to have every bedroom filled with guests and still keep a sense of privacy for your family on the first floor. I'll show you how to do that," Granny said as she climbed the back doorsteps to the upper level.

"See. This back entrance will be for your guests. Perhaps, the only people who will ever come to the front entrance will be your family; personal friends; and of course, some newcomer needing help."

She walked down the hallway, pointing out bedrooms, closets, bathrooms, and the number of beds, cots, and pull-out sofas. "If need be, you can sleep at least 30 people here at one time," she said.

"Oh, my," Judith said. "Did you ever have that many at one time?"

"Only two or three times," Granny said, "but we fared fine."

"How did you happen to have so many?" Judith asked.

"Well, one time I remember we had a freak, flash flood that drove some people from their homes. Another time, there was a power outage during the coldest part of winter. Fortunately, we still had electricity and heat. I really think bad storms sent the most people here; but usually, they didn't have to stay long."

When Judith uttered another, "Oh, my," Granny said, "Don't worry, child. I've seen you in action. You and Scott are up to the job."

"I surely hope so," Judith said under her breath.

Days later, Judith was to remember this conversation and wonder if these words were a forewarning of things to come.

Every plan for Scott and Judith's wedding was falling into place perfectly. Judith constantly marveled at the ease she was having checking off details that usually took months of planning. She could hardly wait for the July date. Everything was ready.

Then came the tragedy that affected 15 families in the Zilford Community Church and hundreds of others. The disaster happened so very quickly and with almost no warning.

No rain had fallen for three weeks. Plants and even shrubbery drooped over parched, cracked ground. Famers and gardeners prayed and cried for rain. Perhaps, that is why they welcomed the black clouds that rolled overhead, darkening the sky at midday.

It was not until the joyful, sky watchers saw an ominous black funnel forming in the distance that they despaired, frantically grabbing family members and pets to race for some form of cover. Absolutely no one in their locality had storm shelters. Why should they? Tornados had never, in the history of Zilford, threatened their rolling-hill area!

Inside their homes, screamers crouched in the centermost section of their dwellings, covering their ears as the deafening roar of a thousand trains roared over them.

Icy water thrashed huddled bodies as their crumbling houses were sucked up above. whirled away, and plunked down 50 yards away. For a three-mile swath, the raging storm leapfrogged, splintering anything in its path.

A momentary, eerie silence replaced the deafening roar that steadily raged angrily away, still demolishing anything in its path.

Then came the moans, the sobbing, the screams as drenched or blood-splattered survivors struggled to crawl from their demolished homes to gaze dumfounded upon heartbreaking destruction.

It had taken only minutes for the monstrous twister to demolish 38 homes – 15 belonging to Zilford's church members.

Hansley Haven, the Zilford Community Church, and the parsonage had been spared, but sorrow was felt immediately; for frantic calls poured in, informing the Pastor of devastating losses affecting the church family.

Using his cell phone, Scott raced toward the Haven, encouraging Judith and Granny to be ready. He asked them to accompany him to the destroyed homes to help minister to the grieving families.

Four blocks away from the stricken area, the three were halted by National Guardsmen who explained, "Power lines are down."

Someone who recognized Scott added, "Pastor, no one, except technicians, can go in yet. It's not safe. Stay here." Pointing, he said, "The Red Cross is going to set up a tent on that lot; and we'll be bringing (he started to say 'the wounded,' but changed his wording) people here. Park over there," he said indicating a driveway that led to the crumbled foundation of a home.

Scott wheeled his car to the designated spot, put his head down on the steering wheel, and said, "Let's pray. Let's pray for these heartbroken people."

Men and women, concerned about their loved ones, hovered around the edge of the Red Cross tent, watching as doctors and nurses tended to distraught people, who like zombies, yielded to instructions, sitting or lying where they were directed. Only whimpering crying was heard. Once in a while, a child cried uncontrollably when blood was washed away from a cut or when a shot was given. Adults, for the most part, grimaced and bore pain without sound.

Scott and his two helpers moved quietly among the shivering onlookers, giving a hug or a warm pat on the back to those who clung together crying or to those who stood erect with glaring, non-seeing eyes, too shocked to process what was happening.

Bringing victims in safely took several hours. Electrical engineers moved like snails among downed trees and wiring, carefully seeking to assess and eliminate danger. Those trapped in partial homes stared, like caged animals, through splintered openings and begged for help.

"Stay where you are," they were told. "When it's safe, we'll have you out of there. Do what you are told. Do not leave where you are. Electrical wires are down."

Because of the response to these engineers' authoritative commands, only one electrocution had been reported. Commander Harrell had been there when it happened. He was edging toward a home draped in fallen electrical lines. From the side of the house, suddenly a white-haired, old man stumbled into the yard, shouting back to his wife who pleaded for him to him to come back.

"No, no, no!" he cried . "I can't, Lori! I can't! I'd rather die!"

As he zigzagged across the lawn, his soaked clothing became entangled with hidden wires, wires that came alive, snapped, and sputtered fire. Without a screech or a groan, the old man toppled to the ground, jerked erratically, quivered, and then lay still, his eyes bulging and his tongue drooping from his mouth.

The Commander yelled to his assistant. "Talk to that woman!

Now! Talk to her. Be sure she doesn't come out. Tell her I'm sending for help." He gave the command, knowing that help would be futile.

He flipped his phone and contacted the Red Cross personnel. "Are any ministers there?" he asked.

"Yes, Sir. I can see the ministers from the Baptist, Methodist, and Community Churches They're talking with the Rabbi. Which one do you want?"

"Wait. Let me check the address. This should be 501 Lyon Avenue. See which minister has someone living here."

In response to the address, Scott Jacobs rushed forward. "Oh, dear Lord," he whispered when he learned what had happened. "That must be Jake Jennings. Poor Jake has always been so cursed with a phobia that he could not stand any tight places. Our church always arranged for him to sit near a window or glass door.

As he mounted the jeep that waited for him, he said to the driver. "Poor Jake. He's 80, you know. He probably couldn't stand the cramped, inner space that they took him to for safety. Dear, dear Mildred. She must be out of her mind."

The driver said, "Let's just hope she doesn't try to go to him until the current's off."

When the jeep crept to a stop, Scott could see the way had been cleared and that the Commander was standing helplessly by, watching a little gray-haired woman hovering over her husband's cold body.

In seconds, the pastor was holding the sobbing wife, trying to give her comfort.

At times, stretchers were needed for persons suffering broken bones or internal injuries. Often, however, the mere guidance of a trained paramedic or guardsman sufficed as disoriented, glazed-eyed survivors staggered into the Red Cross shelter.

Once again, Pastor Scott was called upon to go to one of his beloved members. He knelt by frail Mr. Swinson who, in confusion, still cowered on his water-soaked, closet floor, refusing to leave.

"Brother Swinson," Scott said. "This is your pastor. I'm here to take you to a good, safe place. Your family wants to see you. How 'bout letting this good man here help me get you out of here. Will you do that?"

The elderly, dazed man searched the pastor's face. When a flicker of recognition crossed his countenance, Scott spoke to him, "See, Brother Swinson. I'm your pastor. I'm here to help you. Are you ready to go?"

Noting a slow nod, Scott slipped his arm under Mr. Swinson's arm pit and slowly helped the trembling, 92-year-old man to his feet. With a guardsman on the other side, Scott eased his oldest member from the rubble and led him toward the tent.

Dusk was falling when the last saddened people stumbled toward the medical station. Only several anxious family members remained, standing close to each other to fend off the cold wind that whipped under the tent. As they talked quietly, they sipped the Red Cross coffee, mainly so that they could wrap their numb fingers around warm Styrofoam cups.

Scott slipped to Judith's side, brushed a straggling wisp of hair behind her ear, and whispered. "Thank you for all your help, my little Judy. You're going to make a wonderful preacher's wife. That is, if you still want to be a preacher's wife. Today, you got a taste of what you might be in for. Again, he asked her, 'Do you think you want to submit yourself to this type of life?' Are you sure you want to be a preacher's wife?"

She did not hesitate to answer. "Of course, I want to be a preacher's wife, not just any preacher's wife, you know. I want to be the wife of Scott Jacobs…to work by his side for the rest of my life. I believe God has ordained it."

He wanted to kiss her and in spite of the few lingering people, he might have dared to do so; but at that moment, the guardsmen trudged forward with a family of four needy people.

Before heading to assist them, Scott touched Judith's arm and said, "Honey, you do know, however, that we can't get married in July now. We're going to be needed for a few weeks. Our wedding plans will have to be on hold."

She blinked back tears and tried to smile as she nodded her head.

Chapter 27

Because of the disaster, every room in Hansley Haven was filled. Judith had given up her bedroom and moved across the hall to Granny's room, making space for a couple and their six-month old baby. All upstairs space was occupied – sometimes four to a room; and eight teenage boys, with sleeping bags, had been bedded down in the sun room.

One displaced family with four children, ranging in ages between three months and eight years old, was staying in the parsonage with Scott. Five- year-old, boy twins skidded over his hardwood floors, sometimes yanking Scott's pants and playing tag around his legs. In spite of all the noise and confusion twins Chad and Brad caused, the boys' parents seemingly did not hear or see anything they did. They never lifted their eyes or voiced corrections. Even more troublesome to Scott, the mother, seemingly unmindful of his presence, exposed herself as she cradled her nursing baby. Embarrassed, Scott turned his head quickly and spoke to the father who sullenly continued bouncing a toddler on his knees without responding.

The pastor soon found he welcomed calls that took him away from home, day or night. His heart truly went out to his distraught visitors, and he longed to give them absolute freedom;

yet, his 28 years had not prepared him for a full-blown family all at once, especially a huge, dysfunctional one.

Is this the way it will be for Judith and me? he thought as he sought refuge in his car. *I've been worrying about Judith, but the question should be, 'Will I be up to the job?'*

Each "housed" family had been asked to fill out a registration sheet, listing adult and children's names, their clothing sizes, personal needs, and medicines. The church's Benevolence Committee had gathered the lists and quickly set out to find ways to meet specific needs.

Families from Zilford's hardest hit section fearfully awaited the guardsmen's word that they could return to their homes to assess the damage and to salvage anything that could be salvaged.

"Oh, Pastor, when will it be?" elderly Molly Emerson sobbed. "I don't know whether my cat and dog are alive. They were not in the house with me. I don't know where they are. Oh, Pastor, I need to get home!"

"Yes, you do," Scott said, "and it won't be long now. Mrs. Emerson, I bet the first thing you'll see will be those pets of yours, safe and sound. Just wait and see."

Scott, his associate pastor, and Caleb moved from one family to another, seeking to encourage young and old. In addition, volunteer church members had been assigned to each home to help in searches for things that could be salvaged. Judith checked the lists that had been distributed and noted that she, Granny, and one of the church's secretaries had been assigned to the home of Peter and Marcia Summerfield. She was pleased.

Since meeting the Summerfield's son, Paul, at the backyard event earlier in June, Judith had longed to talk with adoptive parents Peter and Marcia. She didn't want to be nosey but she wanted to know more about Paul's stay at the Haven and about his adoption into the Summerfield Family. Now, she would have time to talk with all of them. It saddened her heart, however, that this meeting had to be in such a grim situation.

The day the almost-annihilated community was officially reopened brought both joy and grief - - joy because families hoped to find their sacred belongings - - grief because the sight of their homes in shambles drove them into overwhelming shock.

Judith, Granny, and Nancy stood apart from the Summerfields, hugging each other and crying as they watched the heartbroken family huddle together in disbelief. A part of their ranch styled home had been ripped off, taking the entire kitchen, gutting the dining room, and leaving an ominous, gaping hole into the other part of the house.

Pastor Scott stood with his left arm propped over the side of Peter Summerfield's pickup truck. Peter leaned heavily against the truck and said, "Pastor, I've always claimed Romans 8:28 that **'All things work together for good to them that love the Lord';** but, for the life of me, I can't see how this can work any good for my family."

"Brother Peter, you're right. We can't always see how God is working things out. I suppose there'll be some things we'll never understand until we get to heaven. We just have to trust our Lord for the outcome He has promised those who love Him."

Peter stood silent for a few moments, watching his wife pick up a dripping object from the rubble. He said, "Pastor, look at my Marcia. You know what an optimist she is? Scott nodded. "Well, do you know what she said when she saw our house fifteen minutes ago? In moments, she brushed the tears from her face and said, 'Well, Peter Summerfield, I have been wanting to redo my kitchen for months. I don't have to bug you anymore. It looks as though God and the insurance company are going to take care of things for me.' I tell you, Pastor, I had to laugh in spite of everything."

At that time, young Paul Summerfield's car crunched to a stop on the cracked driveway.

"Hi Pastor," Paul said, coming forward and extending his hand. Then he said, "How's it going, Dad? How's Mom doing?"

"Well, Son, I was just telling the pastor your mother's reaction to our half-standing home." He placed his arm over his son's shoulder and told him what Mrs. Summerfield had said. Then all three men burst out laughing, causing the women to stop their slow, layer-by-layer searching.

"Peter Summerfield, what are you doing? What on earth can be funny at a time like this?"

"You, my dear," he said. "You."

Rolling her eyes, Marcia Summerfield turned back to the pile of soaked sheet rock and tangles of curtains and broken china. She gave a yank and then cried out. Blood spurted from her hand as she held it up above her head.

"Oh, dear, look what I've done," she cried as the men raced toward her, and Nancy placed her arm around Marcia's waist while examining the cut.

Nancy turned to Judith and said, "Judith, reach in my pocket and get my key. Run across the street to the duplex on the left. That's mine. Go in and get a bottle of Peroxide and some bandages from my medicine cabinet."

Judith gazed at the untouched duplex building as she began moving away. *How odd that some structures were demolished and others stood unscathed.*

"Judith," Nancy yelled as Judith crossed the street, "look in the top drawer of the chest in my bedroom and bring that tube of Neosporin.

Inside, Judith grabbed the Peroxide and bandages and hurried into the adjoining bedroom. She spied the tall, mahogany chest and shifted her supplies to her left hand so that she could open the top drawer.

She had touched the tube of ointment when her eyes fell upon a picture – a picture that took her breath away. She lifted the photograph of a baby, dressed in blue pajamas with elf-like toes. Almost fearful, she turned the picture and read, "My precious baby – Born July 9, 1956. The date rang a bell.

She did not know why, but she slipped the picture into her coat pocket.

Chapter 28

Granny and Judith were the first to arrive at the church; that is, not counting the pastor. He was there, of course, to greet them and to steer them into the conference room. Judith had glanced into this meeting room before in passing, but she had never been inside. Usually, the conference room was used for Deacons' and Board Members' meetings. Smaller counseling groups met in the offices of various staff members.

"You, two, sit here," Scott said, indicating the chairs to the right of his accustomed seat at the head of a huge, mahogany table that could easily seat 14 people.

Granny said, "Pastor, does that mean that Judith and I are your right-hand men?"

He laughed. "You have that right, Granny. I couldn't do without either one of you."

Judith scanned the room, admiring the décor. Soft beige, satin-striped wallpaper covered the lower wall up to the white chair railing. The upper walls, reaching to the vaulted ceiling, bore only the slightest tint of beige. A narrow, oblong table with an elaborate flower arrangement of yellow and orange mums graced the opposite wall. She admired two gold-rimmed pictures of rustic scenery. Reaching down to slide her hands over the plush chair cushions, she marveled at the relaxed atmosphere the entire room induced.

Hearing someone entering the hallway, Scott arose and went to the door. "Hello, Nancy," he said. "Come right in and take a seat by Granny."

As the church's executive secretary, Nancy usually knew minute details of whatever was going on in the Community church, but this called meeting had baffled her. She took a seat and whispered to Granny, "What's this all about?"

Surprised, Granny said, "You don't know? I thought you were the one who knew everything the pastor had on his calendar."

"Usually I do," Nancy said, "but I don't recall talking with him about this meeting. When he called and told me he wanted Judith and me here at 7 o'clock, I just said, 'Yes, Sir. We'll be there.' I did ask, 'Do you want me to take notes?' and he said, 'Not this time, Nancy' and that was all."

The pastor was in the hallway, still greeting people and leading them to the conference room. When he finally closed the door and took his seat, the group gazed upon each other, trying to understand the strange selection of people gathered together. In addition to Granny, Judith, and Nancy, there were Peter and Marcia Summerfield, their son, Paul, and his wife, and Felix Finimore, the church's Attorney at Law who was not a member of their church.

Scott shuffled a few papers and glanced slowly around the table before beginning, "Folks, I know you are trying to figure out why I've called you here; so, let's have prayer and get started."

He prayed, asking for wisdom, guidance, and blessings upon all in the room.

Clearing his throat, the pastor said, "Everyone in this room, including Mr. Finimore, knows that Paul was adopted by the Summerfields when he was four years old." Paul and his parents moved forward in their seats with questioning frowns upon their faces. Color crept to Paul's cheeks and he said, "Is this meeting about me?"

The pastor smiled and said, "Well, yes, you might say that. You know there are certain things you have talked with me about. As a matter of fact, at times every person in this room has asked me similar questions." There were a few shrugged shoulders but no comments. The Pastor took time to give full attention to Paul. "Paul" he said, "you know you were a blessed little boy even if you were left at Hansley Haven as a mystery bundle, for the Hansleys loved you as their own, immediately, and for the four years you were entrusted to their care." Paul gave a nod and faint smile.

The Pastor continued, "Paul, it was on your fourth birthday that the Summerfields came forward and asked to adopt you. Mr. Finimore was called in, and the rest has become history. You officially became the Summerfield's son. Over the years, they have loved you and brought you up in the nurture and admonition of the Lord. They have seen you through school and college and watched you become a pillar in our church, as well as a respected CEO in the Harpo Accounting Firm."

"For that, I'm very thankful," Paul said, reaching over and patting his mother's hand and giving a slight salute to his dad. Mr. and Mrs. Summerfield sat on the edge of their chairs, forcing their tight lips into smiles.

"During your teen years," the pastor continued, "the Summerfields told you repeatedly that they would never object if you sought to find your birth parents. Since I've been your pastor, you have privately expressed to me that someday you would like to pursue that search. Well, I'm happy tonight to be able to give you the information you need."

No one moved. It was as though all even dared to breathe.

"Paul," the pastor said, "Do you have that baby picture you have always carried in your billfold?"

"I surely do," Paul said, reaching into his pocket. He removed the picture and handed it to the pastor who looked at it and passed it to the person next to him. As the passing continued, each person looked at the photograph and smiled.

"Paul, I have another picture similar to this one. I surely hope someone will forgive my good, upright, soon-to-be wife; for, to be honest, she swiped this picture."

He held up an almost identical picture – a baby dressed in blue pajamas with elf-like footies. He turned over one of the pictures and read, "Born July 9, 1956."

Someone gasped as he turned over the other picture and read, "My precious baby. Born July 9, 1956."

Paul stood. "Pastor, whose picture did Ms. Judith swipe? Pastor, do you know where Ms. Judith got that picture?"

The pastor didn't have to answer, for Secretary Nancy Gibbins burst into tears. She turned and pressed her face onto Granny's shoulder.

In a second, Paul was by Nancy's chair, kneeling. "Ms. Nancy! Ms. Nancy, are you my birth mom? Are you my birth mom?"

For an answer, Nancy threw her arms around Paul's neck and sobbed.

Judith had wondered about the box of Kleenex on the table. Now, she knew why they had been placed there. Everyone was crying, even the lawyer.

......

After the initial shock had slowly ebbed, the group seemingly collapsed in their cushioned seats and waited for Paul and Nancy to finish their communication.

With his elbows resting on Nancy knees, Paul said, "Ms. Nancy. I don't know what to call you now. You've always been

Ms. Nancy to me, and I've always loved you. When I was growing up, you babied me and always gave me whatever I wanted."

Nancy's eyes flashed, "But I whacked your backside when you acted up, remember?"

Paul laughed and gave her a hug. "I should thank you for that. I'm sure I needed it."

"Oh, no," Nancy came to his defense, "You were always a good boy."

Paul studied Nancy's face as though he was seeing it for the first time. He said, "I call my mother 'Mom.'" He looked at Mrs. Summerfield. "Mom, what shall I call my birth mom?"

"Why not 'Mother?'" Mrs. Summerfield said without hesitation. "I'm Mom to you, and she can be Mother. After all, everyone in Zilford has always known you were adopted. Our church people will be happy to know you've found your birth mother, and will they ever be surprised!" she said, laughing and covering her mouth.

Judith stood and said, "Here, Paul," turning her chair, "you sit here beside (she started to say Ms. Nancy) but changed it to 'your mother.' Sit in my chair; I'll take your place."

With their chairs facing each other and their knees touching, Nancy and Paul, still holding hands, seemingly became oblivious to everyone else as they began to talk.

"Mother," Paul said with deliberation, "I want to ask you some questions. You don't have to answer them if you don't want to." He took a deep breath. "Do you mind telling me why you left me at Hansley Haven when I was a baby? Were you alone? Didn't I have a father?"

"Oh, Son, you don't know how many times I've wanted to tell you why you were left and to tell you about your dad. He was a wonderful man and you would have loved him."

"Tell me, Mother. Tell me now."

Everyone eased forward to listen.

"Son, your father was a military man. When he came home from his last tour of duty overseas, he became very ill. At first, we thought he had bad colds or the flu, but we learned at the VA that he had contracted tuberculosis. In time, the VA determined to send him to a sanitarium out west to a dryer climate. You were a baby; and, honestly, I feared for your constant exposure to tuberculosis. At the same time, I knew your father was very sick and he needed me. He and I agonized over our decision. It broke our hearts to leave you, but both of us knew it was the best thing to do." She wiped her eyes. "We had checked out the Hansley's home very carefully and knew you would get excellent care, something that we could not give you at that time. We planned to come back for you when your father got well; but unfortunately, he didn't get well. He gradually became worse. I took a job at the hospital so that I could be near him. It was a long, hard fight, but your dad died. He was only 35 years old. It was then that I came back to Zilford. You had been adopted by the Summerfields and seemed to be so very happy. Again, I was forced to do what I thought was best for you. I got a job at the church and rented the duplex across the street from your mom and dad. That way, I had the joy of watching you grow up. As a matter of fact, I actually helped you grow up. I always volunteered to babysit for you when you were a toddler.

Mrs. Summerfield exclaimed, "Oh, my, I don't know what I would have done without you, Nancy. Paul stayed at your house almost as much as he stayed at home."

Mr. Summerfield spoke up. "Come to think of it, you gave Paul a birthday party every year. We just thought you were the grandest neighbor anyone could ever have."

There were numerous other remembrances until Paul asked, "Mother, what was my father's name? Am I named after him?"

Nancy seemed stunned by the question. "Oh no, Son. That is a strange thing. You see, I left only your birth date. No name. Let me explain the great thing about your name. When I came back to Zilford and learned that you had been adopted and named Paul Edward Summerfield, I fell on my knees by my bed and thanked the Lord. You know, I couldn't leave a name for you because I planned to come here to live and watch you grow up. As I said, I could only tell your birth date; but, Son, listen to this. Your father's name was Paul Edward!"

With a grin that crinkled every wrinkle on Granny's face, she stood and exclaimed, "Paul, you've got to know this! God, himself, worked everything out. That should prove to you that, from the beginning, He knew you individually." She waved her hands above her head and said, "Hallelujah!"

Mrs. Summerfield stood to say, "You see, Son, all we knew about you was a birth date. We had to give you a name. Let me tell you about how we selected that name. My husband and I considered naming you Moses, you know, because of the basket in the bulrushes, but we decided you might be kidded about that name; so, we went to the New Testament and chose Paul. We chose the middle name, Edward, because my father was named Edward; and since we never had a son of our own, it gave us a chance to let my father have a namesake. And so, you were Paul Edward. My father loved it."

"Listen to that," the pastor said, glancing at Mr. Summerfield. "Remember our conversation earlier today, Peter? Aren't we witnessing some evidences of Romans 8:28?"

Paul turned to the pastor. "Sir, that verse was Ms. Nancy's - that is - my birth mother's favorite verse. She taught me that verse when I was a little boy. He looked into Nancy's eyes, and they said together, *"For we know that all things work together for good to them that love the Lord, to them who are the called according to his purpose."*

Paul and Secretary Nancy stood to hug and hug and hug. The Summerfields happily wrapped their arms around the rejoicing mother and son.

Before she left, Judith slipped close to Secretary Nancy and said quietly, "I'm so very sorry I took the liberty to borrow your picture. Believe me, I've never before wrongfully taken anything in my life. It just was that I saw Paul's billfold picture and I knew how badly he wanted to find his mother. I had to compare the pictures. I immediately took the picture to the pastor and explained. I hope you will forgive me."

"Forgive you? Oh, my dear, I will forever love you for what you have done!" She embraced Judith and danced her around the room for a few seconds.

Chapter 29

The pastor sat in his office, with three opened books on his desk and a legal sized pad of paper, reading and scribbling notes. He grimaced when he heard the secretary's soft rap upon his door. He had, specifically, asked both Lucille and Nancy to run interference for him. Except for an emergency, he did not want to be disturbed. He needed to study.

He steadied himself and called, "Come in."

The door opened and Lucille slipped inside and closed the door. "Pastor, I know you didn't want to be disturbed, but we have a couple here who will not take 'no' for an answer."

"Who is it, Lucille?"

"They told me not to tell you. They want to surprise you," she said timidly.

Seeing Lucille's uneasiness, Scott closed a book and said, "Let them come in, Lucille, and thank you for trying."

As soon as the secretary exited, the door burst open and Caleb Barnett and Debbie Peterson did a "ta-da" entrance, giggling like teenagers. Scott had to laugh.

"What's with you two?" he asked.

Caleb said, "Congratulate me, Pastor. I asked Debbie to marry me and she said, 'yes!'"

After the initial excitement of hugs and congratulation, Scott went behind his desk and flopped into his chair "Well, that's great! Now, do you two want to tell me something about your plans?"

"Do we ever?" Caleb said, laughing and putting his arm around Debbie's shoulder. You see, for us to get married, we need a favor from you."

"And…from Judith, too," Debbie added.

"What kind of favor? What is it that you want? How can the two of us help?"

Caleb took a deep breath and then began a long spiel that he must have rehearsed many times. "You see," he said, "I have another year in graduate school. Debbie and I don't want to wait a year. We want to get married. We want to get married right away. We really don't have much money and we don't have much time before the new semester begins."

He took a breath and continued, "We know you and Judith have had to reset your new wedding date to August 10. That date would be perfect for us!"

A puzzled expression covered Scott's face as he edged forward on his chair.

"Now, Judith and Debbie have all the same friends," Caleb said.

For the first time, Debbie interrupted, "I may have a few college friends and Caleb may have a few extra friends…"

"But, Scott, both of us think we have a great solution to our needs. We want to see if we can get married the same time you do? You have all the plans made. Dr. Hudson is my professor, too, and I'd love having him conduct my wedding. I know you've already paid for everything and Lucille and Nancy have everything under control," Caleb continued.

Once again, Debbie chimed in. "I know Judith is wearing her mother's wedding gown and I'm wearing my mother's. Everything's just perfect!"

Scott sat speechless, feeling that someone had socked him in the gut.

"Wouldn't a double wedding be great?" Caleb said. "Our church would love it!"

Scott stood and started pacing the floor. "Now, it's not that I'm against what you're planning; but, surely, you know I can't make this decision without consulting Judith. The wedding's a big thing with a girl. As for my part, I'd almost rather elope, but don't tell her I said that!"

"We know that Judith will need to okay the plan, but we need your consent first; then we'll go to her."

"You're not planning that old spin we used when we were kids: 'Mom, I want to ask you, but Dad has said it's all right if you agree,' are you?"

"No, no, we won't do that. As a matter of fact, we want you to go with us so that you can see, first hand, Judith's reaction."

Scott sat back down and placing his elbow on the desk, cupped his face. "This has to be the most brilliant or the most stupid plan I've ever heard. I have no idea what Judith will say."

"Well, I happen to know she's home right now," Debbie said. "Can you go with us to run this by her?"

Feeling sick at his stomach, Scott closed the other two opened books on his desk and turned over the legal pad. *What else can I do?* He left his desk and immediately found Caleb on his right side and Debbie, on his left, prodding him along.

Judith came to the door with a damp towel wrapped around her head. "Oh my, I didn't know I was going to have company," she said, straightening her sweat shirt and pointing to her turban

"You look beautiful," Scott said. "Anyhow, I really need to see how you're going to look around the house when we're married."

He smiled, but his smile faded when he remembered why they were there.

"Come on in," Judith said, leading them to the den that Granny always used when people came to her home for the first time.

As soon as they were seated, Scott said, "Caleb and Debbie have something they want to run by you." He sank back into the lounge chair and closed his eyes until Caleb started his spiel. *Yes. Just as I thought, he had that speech memorized.*

Through slit eyelids, Scott watched Judith's face. With wide, curiosity-filled eyes, she listened to every word Caleb said, or to the quick remarks made by Debbie.

When the two enthusiasts had said everything that was to be said, they stopped abruptly and with an open-armed "What do you think" gesture, leaned forward.

It was then that Judith did an amazing thing than Scott could never have imagined. Yanking the towel from her hair, she ran to Debbie and Caleb, hugging them and crying, "Yes! Yes! Yes!"

Chapter 30

Since the wedding was scheduled for Saturday, August 10, at four o'clock, days upon days, Zilford Community Church had been the constant tramping ground of interior decorators transforming the huge fellowship hall with swooping gauge drapes and twinkling white lights and with long white-clothed tables bearing center streamers of dark blue satin ribbons glittering with sequins and quarter-sized, crystal nuggets.

Caterers had checked and rechecked the menu and ways to see that the food could be served quickly and properly. Nothing was being left to "chance." Zilford Community Church wanted things perfect for the wedding of their pastor and his intern, Caleb.

Scott strolled through the hallway, speaking to busy workers and thanking them.

"Today's Friday, Pastor. That means you have one last day of freedom," a caterer joked.

"I wish it were today," Scott answered. "I've been trying to get married to this girl for a long time. Something has always seemed to get in the way."

"Well, you won't have to wait much longer, and congratulations!" the man called over his shoulder as he hastened into the kitchen.

Nancy met him as he entered the office. "Pastor," she said, "everything's going along smoothly here. Why don't you go home and try to rest? We'll call you if we need you. Remember, you don't have to preach Sunday. You'll be on your honeymoon."

"I will," he answered with a gleam in his eyes. "Nancy, it looks as though it's actually going to happen. Maybe, I can stop holding my breath."

They both laughed, thinking of Scott and Judith's rocky courtship.

"You know, Nancy, I believe your advice is good. I think I will go home and check out my tuxedo. I'd better be sure it fits."

"Yes, you'd better be sure. If you don't mind my saying so, Pastor Scott, I know you're going to be a handsome groom."

"Thank you, dear Nancy. How would I ever do without you?"

He took one last look at his cleared-off desk, flipped off the light, closed the door, and hummed "God is So Good" as he headed for his car.

Later, he stood before the floor-length mirror and gazed at himself dressed in a white tuxedo, ruffled shirt, maroon cummerbund, and matching bow tie. He grinned, comparing this outfit with his former staid, navy blue suits and conservative ties.

"You know," he said aloud. "I believe Nancy is right. I'm going to make a handsome groom. At least, I hope Judith thinks so."

He had just hung his tuxedo up when the phone rang. He answered and heard his mother say, "Son, we're on our way, but we just heard something on the news. I don't know whether it will pertain to you or not, but your brother thinks that Joshua Peterson is attending Camp Keeawana this week."

"Yes, he is. He's coming home tomorrow morning. What could pertain to Joshua?"

"Well, Son, it seems that today the campers were making that last-day Appalachian climb, the one you always made when you went to camp."

"I remember that climb," Scott said. "It was a rough one."

"I know, but something unusual has happened. It seems the counselors returned to camp without realizing that two of the boys were not with them. Since noon, the rangers have been checking and are now sending out search teams. This may have nothing to do with you or the Petersons. There were only two boys and it's not likely one is Joshua, but I wanted to check with you."

"Thank you, Mom. I'll call right now." Once again, Scott felt a knotting in his inner being.

As soon as Mrs. Peterson answered the phone, he knew by the quiver in her voice that, without doubt, Joshua was one of the missing boys!

"No, Scott," Caleb said. "You do not need to go. I'm going with the Petersons. Keeawana is only two hours away. We still have lots of daylight, and I'm sure we'll find the boys. All of us should be back before bedtime." He laughed nervously, "You know, we have a big day ahead of us tomorrow."

"I hope so," Scott said, remembering the roller coaster ride he and Judith had taken since the day they met. "At any rate, Caleb, I'm on my way to see the Petersons. I'll make my decision after I've talked with them."

"That sounds good," the young intern said. "See you soon."

Before Scott could park his car, Mr. Peterson came out onto the porch to wait for him. "Pastor," he said, "We know you've come to offer to go with us; but, really, we'd like it if you would stay here and keep everything moving along. We don't feel we're going to have trouble finding the kids. Many of us have been on that hike before, and we'll know where to look."

Scott gave his friend a hug and said, "If that's what your family wants, Sir, I'll stay here and see that everything is readied for tomorrow."

Mrs. Peterson came onto the porch. She gratefully accepted a hug and comforting words from Scott before saying, "I've just talked with your secretary. All prayer groups have been notified. I'm sure the Lord is hearing many prayers for Joshua and his friend right now. They're going to be all right, Pastor. I know it in my heart."

"I'm sure they will be." He noticed Debbie headed to the car with a few canvas bags and hurried to help load the car. "You folks need to get on the road. You know, we want you back and in bed before midnight. Wedding bells are going to ring tomorrow."

Scott did not leave until he had prayed with Caleb and the Petersons and had watched them ride out of sight.

The wait during the rest of the day was torturous. In every room of his house, Scott kept a television or radio dialed to a news station. No matter where he moved or what he was doing, he could hear frequent reports about the missing teens. At five o'clock, he received a call from Caleb.

"Scott, we're here. Mr. Peterson and I are heading out to search right now. The concern is to find the boys before dark. They both were wearing short sleeved shirts and, I don't need to tell you, it gets cold here in these mountains at night. I won't mention the other dangers if they're still in the woods when it's dark. Pray for us."

Scott checked and double checked every detail of the wedding plans: the ceremony lineup, the receiving line plan, the catering, and the honeymoon getaway. As the hours dragged by, his heart grew heavy. He knelt by his bed and prayed: "Father, I've waited so very long for the time I could make Judith my wife. Both of us love you and want to serve you. Would you, please, take control of this situation." He cried as he prayed for Caleb and Debbie and for the search parties. Still in his kneeling position, he slumped his head onto the bed and fell asleep.

At nine o'clock, Scott was jarred awake by the phone's ring. In the darkened room, he stumbled to turn on a light and snatch the telephone. As soon as he lifted the receiver, he heard Caleb yelling, "We've found them! We've found them! They're okay. A search team is bringing them in now. Hey, Scott! Scott, are you there? Did you hear what I said? We've found the boys! We'll be home before midnight. Nothing's going to turn into a pumpkin tonight! Have to go! See you, Pal."

Paul flopped backward onto the bed, fully dressed, and mumbled "Thank you, Lord" over and over until he fell into a deep sleep.

A loud tapping on his bedroom window aroused him. "Scott! Scott, are you in there?" he heard his father calling.

Disoriented only for a moment, he answered, "Yeah, Dad, I'm here. I'll be right there to let you in." He groped through the darkness to the front door.

His excited family filed in, smothered him with hugs and well wishes, and ordered him back to bed. In less than an hour, the whole Jacobs' Clan had made it to their usual sleeping quarters and had succumbed to the sleep they needed to prepare them for the big day.

CHAPTER 31

Judith called early Saturday morning. "Honey," she said, "I know we can't see each other today, but I just wanted to hear your voice. I'm in a dream world. I can hardly believe today I will finally become Mrs. Scott Jacobs."

"I can hardly believe it either. Yesterday, for a while there, I had my doubts."

"Scott," Judith said softly, "I dare say you and I will be the only couple to have a really big wedding without a rehearsal."

"I know and that scares me, but it couldn't be helped."

"I guess it won't matter to anyone if we goof up a little."

"Don't worry, Judith, you and I can wing it. I've conducted 20 weddings so far, and I think I know what you and I are supposed to do. Nancy and Lucille have printed the whole procedure precisely. They've given these plans to the wedding party, and I'm confident we have smart family members and attendants who can follow written instructions."

"Yes, and there's Dr. Hudson. He'll guide us."

"Dr. Hudson. That reminds me. I'm having lunch with him at noon. I think I'd better step on it. I can't be late, you know."

"No, and don't you dare be late at four o'clock."

Scott laughed. "My dear, neither wild beasts nor raging storms could keep me away today at four o'clock."

Someday, I might laugh at the irony of my words, but not today,
Scott thought as he rushed down the hospital corridor. Shortly
after one o'clock, he had received a frantic call from Mrs. Dunbar,
a widowed young woman who was bringing up an eight-year-
old boy.

"Pastor," she cried. "Please come! Please come. I need you
to pray for Gregory. He's been attacked by two pit bulldogs.
They've chewed his leg. They've hurt my son! Oh, Pastor, please
come."

As he rushed to the hospital, Scott talked with hospital
personnel by phone and learned that, fortunately, the bites were
superficial. They would have been worse if the boy had not been
wearing heavy jeans and if a mailman had not kicked the dogs
away.

"The mother is very distraught, however," the nurse said.
"Your presence will help calm her down. We're glad you're on
your way. We know about your wedding today, Dr. Jacobs, and
we'll get you back as quickly as possible."

"Thank you," Scott said, once again thinking that sometimes
he liked living in a small town where everybody knew everything
that was going on with everyone.

It was 3:30. Only thirty minutes to go. Surrounded by
boisterous groomsmen strutting around in tuxedos and admiring
themselves in the mirrors, Scott felt an urge to go to the window
to check the weather. He breathed a sigh of relief, for the summer
sky was blue with only a few clouds in sight.

At least, I didn't put a whammy on the weather he said to himself
as he took his tux from the hangers and started to the adjoining
room to dress.

He was tucking his shirt into his pants when Dr. Hudson
spoke, "I say, Scott, someone did some good planning when

this church was laid out. I like the way the groom's party is on one side with these two rooms and bathroom facilities and the bride's party has similar facilities on the other side. It's private and convenient."

"Yes, I like it, especially today. It's good to be in this room just with you and Caleb right now. Those guys in the other room are really keyed up."

Dr. Hudson, noting Scott's jitters, said, "Son, I think that's a lot like the pot calling the kettle black."

Scott responded with a nervous laugh.

On the bride's side, in one room bridesmaids sat before a wall with six mirrored vanities and combed their hair or checked their makeup. Others stood before two floor-length mirrors, admiring their shimmering, satin gowns, navy blue sashes, and gold-colored shoes.

In the adjoining room, Judith and Debbie were getting final inspections by Mrs. Johnson and Mrs. Peterson. The mothers had dressed early, hoping to give their daughters last-minute help.

"I remember how nervous I was when I wore this dress," Mrs. Johnson said to Judith as she buttoned a row of pearls on the sleeves. I had to get my mom to do the buttoning. I couldn't seem to make my fingers work."

Mrs. Peterson was fluffing the long satin skirt on Debbie's dress. "My problem was this skirt. I kept getting tangled into it when I turned."

Judith and Debbie were not saying much. They were reveling in their mother's memories.

"I'm just so very happy I can wear your wedding gown, Mom," Judith said.

"That goes for me, too," Debbie said to her mother. "I just hope that Caleb and I can always be as happy as you and dad have been.

"I have all the confidence in the world that you will be, Debbie. I believe you're marrying a Godly young man."

Their conversation was interrupted by the maid of honor who stuck her head in the door. "Okay, girls, it's almost time! The church is full of expectant people. You two look beautiful," she said before adding with hesitancy, "I do need to tell you something, Judith."

Judith turned quickly, clasping her hand over her heart. "What? Is something wrong?"

"Don't get excited. It's not much. It's just that Scott does not have any shoes to wear. No one can find his white, patent leather shoes. At first, he thought the guys were playing a trick on him; but then, as the time drew close, he knew they were not. They contacted the Caba Tuxedo Rental; but, unfortunately, they don't have another pair of shoes to fit Scott even if they could get them here in time."

"Can't one of the other men let him have their shoes?" Mrs. Johnson asked.

"They would gladly do that, Mrs. Johnson, but not a single man in either room has feet as big as Scott's. You know he wears a size 13 and is always kidding about his big feet."

"What's he going to do?" Judith asked.

"Well, he hopes you won't mind but he's coming in wearing his white socks. Maybe, no one will notice."

"Well, that's all right," Judith said, "I don't care just as long as we get married. This will just be one more, funny thing we can tell our children and grandchildren."

The maid of honor turned to listen to someone who had nudged her. She turned back and said, "It's time to go, girls. The lineup is beginning."

Before the ceremony began, Dr. Hudson stood on the steps and spoke informally, "Good afternoon, folks. I'm Dr. Hudson, a former seminary professor for both Scott and Caleb. Today, I'll be joining these two young men and their lovely brides in marriage. Ahead of time, I'm going to tell you this may be an unusual service, for as you know, both of these ministers are uniquely gifted and uniquely wired." There was a twitter of laughter.

"In the offset, I need to tell you that Pastor Scott's shoes disappeared; therefore he will be in his stocking feet. I tell you ahead of time so that you will not be shocked. Now, only the Lord knows if there will be other shockers before this service has ended, but we're glad you're here. Just sit back and be blessed."

He looked at his watch. "It's time. Let the wedding begin."

As soon as he had exited, groomsmen seated the two mothers and the organist struck the traditional processional chords.

Although the wedding party had not had an official rehearsal, the director had visited each dressing room and had gone over the plans with both the men and the women. She stood in the foyer and smiled approval as the procession began.

As usual, the officiating minister came out from a door at the front of the sanctuary and took his place in the center of the stage, this time, between two, not one, flower-covered trellises flanked by ornate, candle stands. This time, not one groom, but two entered from the left and took their places, facing the front entrance where the brides would enter.

At first, almost no one paid attention to Scott and Caleb's elegant white tuxedos. Their eyes went immediately to Scott's feet just in time to see him slightly lift his stocking feet and wiggle his toes. The congregation laughed.

Dr. Hudson pressed his lips together for composure and shook his head in amusement.

A groomsman and a bridesmaid, in marked musical time, strolled slowly down the aisle, parted at the center and mounted the steps - she, to the left and he, to the right. The congregation was not sure what was happening until the second couple had positioned themselves. Then they knew. All the men were in their stocking feet. Even Dr. Hudson looked surprised. He remembered how proud the ushers had been of their unusual, white patent leather shoes as they had seated the guests earlier. Now they stood in white socks.

Then the two five-year old ring bearers did a strange thing. They meandered down the long center aisle, going from one side to the other and making growling sounds to whoever was seated on the end seat. It took the audience only minutes to figure out that someone – perhaps, a teen – had told the little fellows that they were ring bears, not ring bearers.

Adults snickered, but tried to keep things under control.

Fortunately, the angelic flower girls obediently eased their way down the white, bridal runway, slightly swinging their baskets and strewing rose pedals.

Suddenly Dr. Hudson, as well as the entire wedding party, were startled by the sound of a trumpet being played from the balcony. They were to learn later that the trumpet solo was the one thing the director had forgotten to mention.

When the last trumpet note was sounded, the organ swelled forth "Here Comes the Bride" and the congregation arose, eagerly awaiting the entrance of the two brides.

Judith Johnson, with eyes aglow, entered the sanctuary, escorted by her uncle. Some dear older lady whispered far too loudly, "Look at Judith Johnson. She's wearing her mama's wedding gown. Ain't that something? She's pretty as a picture."

The audience laughed; but Judith, with her eyes, sought out the speaker and mouthed, "Thank you."

Dr. Hudson shifted from one foot to the other, wondering if he could quell the frivolity of the happy onlookers. He almost gave up, however, when Judith's uncle said, "I'm her uncle on her father's side and so her mother and I do," and Judith came to stand with Scott in front of the left-side trellis. Everything seemed all right until Scott stuck out his foot and wiggled his big toe. He had meant to do so unobtrusively, but too many people saw the gesture. When they noticed Judith's shoulders shaking as she tried to suppress laughter, they quit trying and guffawed. Even Dr. Hudson laughed.

Dr. Hudson lifted his head in a dignified way and waited until there was silence. He nodded slightly to the organist and once again the processional music surged forward.

Escorted by her father, Debbie Peterson glided down the aisle, also beautiful in her mother's dress. Someone sitting near the older woman politely put her finger to her lips and shook her head.

Debbie and Caleb moved to stand before the trellis on the right.

Dr. Hudson motioned for everyone to be seated and moved behind the first trellis to face Scott and Judith. He asked them to turn and face each other. On the right, Caleb and Debbie remained with their backs to the audience until Dr. Hudson came before them and asked them to turn toward each other.

For the rest of the service, Dr. Hudson removed from one trellis to the other, going through the same procedures with each couple. His opening remarks were personalized, mentioning individual things he knew about Scott and Caleb. The prayers, vows, exchanging of rings, and the unity candle ceremony were similar but not identical. Scott and Judith's unity candle was centered in the greenery to their left; Caleb and Debbie's to their right.

Before Dr. Hudson pronounced Scott and Judith 'man and wife,' there was a loud clap of thunder.

Scott said, "Hurry up, Dr. Hudson, get this over. Don't waste time," not thinking Dr. Hudson's mike would pick up his whisper. Everyone laughed

Dr. Hudson said, "I stand to be corrected. You've always wanted to do that, haven't you, young man?"

"No, sir," Scott whispered. "I just want to be sure we get married before anything else happens."

Dr. Hudson said, "And now, by the power invested in me as a minister, I pronounce you, Scott Jacobs, and Judith Johnson 'man and wife.' You may kiss the bride.

As Scott lifted the lacy veil, he said, "Finally!" The audience heard and stood to applaud while Scott held Judith in his arms for a kiss.

Dr. Hudson moved to the right trellis and went through the same procedure just before another clap of thunder was heard, causing Caleb to quickly draw Debbie to himself. Again the congregation stood and applauded as the groom kissed his bride.

Dr. Hudson glowed as he announced the new couples for the first time: "I proudly present to you 'Dr. and Mrs. Scott Jacobs and Rev. and Mrs. Caleb Barnett.'"

Scott and Judith exited first, going up the center aisle and then doing a strange thing. They circled around to the side wall and headed toward the double, opened door that led to the fellowship hallway. Caleb and Debbie followed, doing the same thing.

The Community Church family looked puzzled. They had never seen a wedding done like that before in their church. Usually, the wedding party assembled in the foyer and formed a receiving line.

All attendants followed the leadership of the newlyweds. Groomsmen then came forward and ushered the mothers through the open doorways where the others had gone.

Dr. Hudson, feigned wiping sweat from his brow, and smiled as he said, "Ladies and gentlemen, I'm sure you will agree with me. This was a beautiful, but slightly unusual, wedding. It gives you an idea of what to expect from these two young preachers. I'm sure they're going to lead a happy, progressive church.

"Now, I've been asked to explain this. To make it easy for you to eat a good, hot-cooked meal, the wedding party left in an unaccustomed way, as you surely noticed, in order to form a receiving line for you to go through as you head to the banquet tables. The Jacobs and the Petersons want everyone, and I mean everyone, to join them in the meal. I really wouldn't be surprised if Scott Jacobs hasn't stationed a guard at the front door to keep you from going anywhere except to the fellowship hall.

"Now, before you go, let's praise the Lord for this wonderful occasion and thank Him for the food prepared for us – all of us!"

They heard a burst of laughter coming from the fellowship hall. Dr. Hudson said, "I dare say your pastor just wiggled his big toe."

The End

Printed in the United States
By Bookmasters